FADED GLIMPSES of TIME

FADED GLIMPSES of TIME

NYAH NICHOL

Common Deer Press

Published by Common Deer Press Incorporated.

Copyright © 2022 Nyah Nichol

Published in 2022 by Common Deer Press
1745 Rockland Avenue
Victoria, British Columbia
V8S 1W6

Library of Congress Cataloging-in-Publication Data

Title: Faded Glimpses of Time / Nyah Nichol.
Names: Nichol, Nyah, author.
Identifiers: Canadiana 20210384107 | ISBN 9781988761718 (softcover)
Classification: LCC PS8627.I235 F33 2022 | DDC jC813/.6—dc23

David Moratto, cover and interior design

Printed in Canada

www.commondeerpress.com

*This book is dedicated to all the people
who brought me light and laughter during the pandemic.*

*To name a few:
Dad, Mom, Silas, Everett & Titus
Aryssa and Shaela (coolest sister duo)
Kim (Stacy's Mom)
Aiden (dance battle opponent, fencing expert)
Eric (Romeo & Paris)
Sydney (belay & chicken dance buddy)
Astin (mediumest friend, funniest banana)
Brooke (oldest friend)
Mr. Yoshida's Social Studies class
Mrs. Cherniwchan's Gym class
And my Rockwall family*

PART ONE

WREN DERECHO

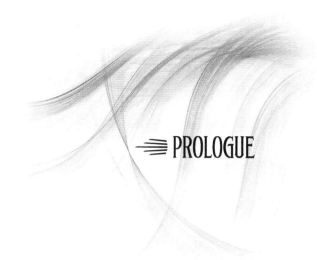

Failure was on the horizon.
Everything was falling apart.
I had made a crucial mistake.
But there was no going back.
I had misunderstood time.
Along with the dimensions it bound us to.
I was unprepared for its anomalies.
I stood, helpless, as my world crumbled apart at the seams.
Nothing could save us now.
It was over.
The orb always won.

October 1, 2059, 3:43 pm...

The time machine disintegrated into wisps of smoke around me, and the floor opened under my feet. I squeezed my eyes shut and clenched my jaw as I plummeted into the darkness. I landed awkwardly on a cold hard surface, sprawled on my side. I winced and imagined the bruise it was going to leave.

My eyes flickered open. I was back in my room, back in my timeline that was hopefully now set on the right course. I had successfully managed to change my future. I saved the timeline and my world from destruction created by the mysterious blue orb and my own villainous tyranny.

"Wren."

I looked at the doorway to see Rob, my guardian and the man who had watched over me for the past two years after my uncle passed away. He cautiously stepped into my room. He was the person I trusted the most, my only family. He also happened to be the security director at a top-secret government organization named DAIR: Department of Advanced Innovation and Research.

Rob couldn't help but notice the state of my room, and, by his expression, I could tell he was in utter disbelief. It looked like a tornado had swept through, tossing debris in every direction. However, my unfinished time machine, Tempus II, stood tall and unscathed. It was the only thing unaffected when the future version of Tempus had opened a portal into my room, triggering the mayhem that lay before us.

Rob quickly recovered from the chaotic sight and chose to disregard the mess for the moment. He turned his attention to me. "I know you've had a difficult time lately, but I want you to know there are people here who really care about you and want to help you."

His eyebrows raised in surprise when I rushed over to embrace him tightly.

My voice shook. "It's over. I'm done with the time machine. I'm done with the orb."

I had left the devious power source in the hand of my friend Alex as the future collapsed all around him. Well, technically, it was Alex's future self who made the heartbreaking but necessary decision not to travel back with me.

Resetting the timeline had cost the lives of my friends. We had grown so close in such a short amount of time, and my heart ached when I recalled the traumatic events that had led to their sacrifice. It was all the incentive I needed to make sure everything progressed the way it was supposed to. I would never let the orb control me or get inside my head again.

As I wondered where Alex would be in this new, altered time, I heard footsteps behind me. "Hi, I'm Alex Donahue."

My pulse quickened at the sound of his voice, and I spun around. Even though I had thought about this moment, it was still a shock to see him younger and not weighed down by stress. He had the same gentle smile and dark hair poking into his eyes, but he seemed lighter and happier in his manner. He was a more innocent version of the man I had met in the future who had endured so much hardship and suffering. I remembered he had the same type of robotics as me, although his mainly worked as leg braces. His left hand was also completely replaced by metal and wires.

I broke away from Rob's embrace. "Wren Derecho."

He walked over and pretended to whisper even though Rob could totally hear him. "I can't believe you locked out Rob. You're pretty crazy, aren't you?"

I laughed as I replied, "You have no idea."

As my eyes met his, my heart skipped a beat, and I inadvertently stumbled backward. My mind struggled to process the shocking difference I hadn't noticed until now.

Trembling, I managed to murmur, "Your eyes are blue."

"What's the matter?" he asked, startled by my odd reaction after having been introduced to him only moments before.

My voice escalated, "Your eyes are BLUE!"

I blinked hard twice, biting down on my parched tongue to wake myself up. I felt my entire body tense up as I realized there was no waking up from this dream. His eyes were perfect mirrors of the orb's deep ocean blue.

"Wren! What's gotten into you?" Rob exclaimed. "Wait...What happened to your face?"

"This isn't right!" I shouted, ignoring his concerns as I recalled my future self.

My older self had those same-coloured eyes after she'd succumbed to the orb's alluring power, and she had ended up being enslaved by it. I had risked everything to destroy that orb.

Did it somehow take control of Alex? Here, in this timeline?

"I stopped the orb. I stopped everything. Your eyes shouldn't be blue," I repeated over and over, but the more I said it, the more my confidence waned. "I abandoned the orb in an alternate collapsing future. It shouldn't be...it can't be...Is it in your head?"

Alex glanced at Rob uneasily, and Rob could only respond with a small shrug and a bewildered expression. He waited a moment for Rob to step in, but noticing that he was at a loss for words, he looked back toward me.

"What are you talking about?" Alex questioned. He spoke in a gentle but confused tone, and his thin lips turned up in a slight, nervous smile. "My eyes have been blue since birth. I know it's an uncommon colour, but you have nothing to be worried about."

His smile was meant to calm me down, but it did just the opposite. It felt like the orb was mocking me.

I took a few deep breaths and gulped down the rising lump in my throat. "In the original timeline, your eyes were hazel."

Rob reached out to put a comforting hand on my shoulder.

"The original timeline? Wren, how would you know what colour Donahue's eyes are? You've never met him until now," he said softly, and I winced. Puzzled, he rubbed the back of his neck. "What's going on? When were his eyes hazel?"

Alex was alive in this timeline—this altered timeline that now felt terribly wrong—but he didn't know me. My face felt warm as a tightness grew in my chest. Even though I knew this would be the situation I was coming back to, I had been unable to prepare myself emotionally. That wasn't even considering the possibility that somehow the orb was still able to manipulate the present reality.

The orb's words that had haunted me throughout my time in the future replayed in my mind, and I suppressed the urge to escape in panic and terror.

You can't fight me...I won't leave you...you'll regret this moment for eternity...you are nothing without me!

I snapped out of my swirling thoughts in numbing disorientation.

Rob tried again, squeezing my shoulder, "Wren, what are you afraid of? If you tell us what's wrong, we can help you."

Even though Alex and Rob were with me, I felt alone and detached from reality.

"Everything is wrong," I muttered.

The thought of the orb's voice returning in my head made me tremble. It had invaded my mind shortly after my arrival to the future and tormented me relentlessly. It had been the one to destroy my future self, and I would never forget the feeling of helplessness as the orb violated my mind, making my own thoughts untrustworthy.

Alex took a step closer, but it only increased my anxiety. For a moment, the image of my future self reaching to pluck the orb out of my grasp flooded my memory. She had taunted me with her supernatural abilities and lethal blue lightning.

"The same lightning could still be coursing through my veins," I reasoned out loud.

Rob and Alex stared at me in stunned silence. Clearly, they thought I was out of my mind. My pulse thundered in my ears, and I dug my metallic fingers into my forehead, attempting to force the traumatic memories out of my mind.

"No, no, no. This can't be happening. It's impossible. The orb was destroyed," I mumbled to myself as I started pacing around the room. Uncontrollable tears welled up in my eyes. "It didn't happen…nothing happened. It's gone. It's over."

Rob pushed up his round, silver-rimmed glasses and repeated, "Wren, slow down and let us help you." He watched me intently, but didn't try to invade my space.

My gaze flicked from Rob to Alex, then to the vast blueprints scattered on the floor, and then back to Alex's worried face. "It makes no sense! Zero sense! It isn't scientifically possible."

Rob straightened up and pulled out a rectangular glass screen from his shirt pocket. "Wren, I'm going to call in some of our specialists from the medical department to take care of you. I'm sorry. I should have gotten you help earlier. You're going to be okay."

"No!" I lunged forward to clamp my robotic fingers on his forearm. "No one can know. You don't understand. I need to protect you…" I glanced at Alex. "And you too. I don't think I stopped it. The orb could destroy everything!"

"Whoa, okay, okay. I hear what you're saying, but regardless of what the orb may or may not do, you need to let someone look at you. We don't have to tell them anything," Rob insisted and gestured toward the door.

I pressed my hands over my eyes in frustration. "What if I made things worse by believing that we could control the timeline? What else is different about this timeline compared to the other one?"

I didn't expect either of them to answer me, and they didn't. Rob reached over to place his hand on my back, but it provided little comfort.

Rob skimmed over the multiple missed messages on his device. "Wren, I don't know what's going on here, but I know it's going to be okay. It's just…right now is not a great time—"

"Rob!" I inhaled deeply, on the verge of sobbing. "I messed things up, and you can't fix it this time. You can't fix me."

I looked down at my robotic hands, remembering waking up in this very facility after the car accident to see the silver metal attached to my broken body. My uncle had fixed me. And after my uncle was gone, Rob had taken care of me. He tried to mend the brokenness in my life. He tried to fix everything I threw at him. But now, things were bigger than the both of us. And it was all my fault.

Rob sighed.

Alex interrupted as he spotted blood soaking through my sleeve, "Your arm…"

I pulled up my sleeve to reveal bits of glass and debris embedded in my upper arm. Surprised, I watched the blood seep from several wounds I had sustained on my harrowing adventure. Gingerly feeling the small gash above my eye, I realized I was a bit of a mess. I became aware of the throbbing pain in my head and the aching muscles in my back and suddenly felt an overwhelming wave of exhaustion wash over me.

My robotic fingers began to emit random sparks, and my metal joints felt stiff from the strain of the last few days. I glanced at the scraped-up battery implant in my wrist. A small red light blinked intermittently. I would need to take care of that soon.

Alex moved his hand toward the cut on my bicep, and, instinctively, I jumped away from him, still feeling agitated. My stomach churned with anxiety. I longed to talk to someone who understood me, but in this timeline, my friends didn't even know me. And if I didn't have them, I would have to face this alone.

Rob slipped his screen back in his pocket, ignoring the incoming messages. "Alex is right. You need medical attention. At least let me help you with that first."

I stared blankly at them, not knowing what to say to convince them I wasn't insane, especially since I wasn't sure of it myself. It was then that Alex noticed the warped safe at the back of my room.

"Rob, look at this." He walked over and ran a finger over the lump of metal that had once been the lock. "What happened here?"

"It was a VU—a vaporizing unit," I blurted, remembering my first encounter with Alex.

He had time travelled from the future to convince me to help him defeat my evil older self. When I'd refused, he zapped the lock to retrieve the orb. According to the rules of time, all of that had happened just minutes ago. But to me, after spending twenty-seven life-changing hours away from this timeline, it seemed like a distant memory.

Rob and Alex exchanged hesitant glances and turned to look at me.

"How did you…?" Rob began.

I hurried over to them.

"It won't be there." I shook my head, then shook it again to convince myself. Knowing the orb couldn't be in the safe calmed my nerves enough for me to speak more reasonably. "I'm not crazy. Rob, if you want the orb, which is why you came here in the first place after we talked outside—wait, that still happened, right?"

"Yes…?"

"So, I think most things are the same, like they were supposed to be in the old timeline…" I thought out loud, then turned toward the safe. "The orb's not there. It no longer exists. I left it in a collapsed future. None of us is ever going to see it again."

The hinges of the safe door creaked as Rob slowly swung it open. I gasped. Inside, the orb radiated its usual hue of blue. An agonizing memory of the otherworldly object, lost until this moment, thrust itself into the forefront of my mind.

Everything happened in the blink of an eye, but I relived it in slow motion.

My dad shielded my mom with his shoulder as she turned her face toward him. The crackling blue lightning rained down from looming dark clouds overhead. My mom's russet hair covered most of her eyes, but I could see her mouth twist into a blood-curdling scream. My dad's emerald-green eyes widened almost comically.

The front of the car had been obliterated. The unnatural lightning seemed to be alive and choosing where to strike. In a split second, my parents were gone forever.

I became aware my seat belt was twisted across my chest, making it difficult to breathe. In agony, I attempted to claw at it, but my fingers—made of flesh, blood, and bone—were useless. I slumped my head back, and a burst of pain shot through my body. There was no escape from the warped skeleton of the car.

I drifted in and out of consciousness. Just before the darkness took over, I caught a glimpse of a glowing blue sphere rolling across the glistening pavement.

9 HOURS and 4 MINUTES to TERMINUS TERRA

October 1, 2059, 4:26 pm…

My jaw fell open at the sight of the orb. My heart skipped a beat before my throat constricted. My breathing turned shallow and painful; it felt like I was suffocating.

The three of us stood in silence for a few long seconds.

I stared at the orb, frozen in place. I was once again unable to tear my gaze from its incandescent beauty. My mind wrestled against something deep and powerful inside me, but, eventually, I broke myself away from its influence.

I snapped my head to the side with immense effort. "Impossible."

"Is that the orb?" Alex asked, intrigued, yet with a hint of recognition in his voice.

I paused before choking out, "Don't touch it! It's not from this world, and it will stop at nothing for power and world domination." My throat felt like sandpaper. "Too much…this is too much."

"So, what are you trying to tell us? You said the orb was gone, but it isn't. Can you start at the beginning?" Rob prompted, trying to be patient.

I swivelled on my heels, tugging on my hair. I felt the colour draining from my face. I wanted to scream. I wanted to cry. I wanted to bolt out of the room, but I couldn't leave them alone with that dangerous object.

Rob continued when I didn't answer him, "Wren, you know how to handle the orb better than any of us. But, like we talked about earlier, I think we should bring it to people who specialize in otherworldly technology and alien power sources. They'll know what to do."

I turned back toward Rob to see him fix his gaze on the safe, his fingers twitching. "Rob, the orb is *my* burden. I can't let anyone else get consumed by its power! You have to understand…you have to trust me."

"What do you mean by 'anyone else'?"

"It got me. I wasn't strong enough. I don't know if I'll ever get rid of it," I grieved, looking up to meet his dark eyes filled with obvious concern.

I inhaled deeply, trying to find the right words. I needed to get my point across, and it was imperative that they saw I was being serious. The tremors shaking my body calmed slightly as I tried to get a grip on my emotions.

"If you allow anyone else to mess with the orb, the results could be catastrophic. Trust me, only I know the extent of its power."

"You know I can't do that," Rob argued.

In the corner of my eye, I saw a flash of metal on the floor. I glanced down and recognized the cracked watch Alex's future version had given me. I must have dropped it.

I snatched it up and held it out. I recalled the engraved words on the back and recited it excitedly, "'*Aut viam inveniam aut faciam*.' I will either find a way or make one…the orb found a way, or it created one that existed outside the boundaries of time and physics…as we know them. It seems impossible."

Wide-eyed, Alex pulled up his sleeve to reveal the original watch on his wrist, minus the cracked face and weathered features. "Where did you get that?"

"From you," I responded.

"How did you…? What…?" he stammered in disbelief. "William Derecho gave me this watch years ago."

"I know."

Rob interjected, pushing up his slipping round glasses again, "Okay, you need to start from the beginning, Wren."

"I don't know where to start. Tempus III…the orb…my evil, insane future self as a superpowered dictator…" I rambled, waving a hand at the pyramid-shaped machine and the safe before I stopped myself.

I took a moment to gather my thoughts, and then gestured toward one of the tables where we could sit down. Before any of us could take a step, we were interrupted by a middle-aged lady rapping her knuckles on the already-opened door. She was dressed in a gray suit and had almond-shaped eyes framed by horn-rimmed glasses. Silver streaks peppered her sleek black hair.

"I'm sorry for interrupting," she said, clearly not sorry at all. "Director Mallick, we've been waiting for you in the control centre. Do you need to get your TetraScreen looked at? I don't think my messages are coming through."

Rob turned away from us as the lady briskly walked out. Even the click of her heels echoing in the hallway sounded annoyed. He fished out his TetraScreen and shot a glance at Alex.

"What's going on?" I asked. "Who was that?"

He hesitated before explaining, "Oh…it's nothing. Um, just an upcoming mission: Operation Aquarius Deep. That was the Director of DAIR, Everlyn Li. Basically, my boss. I would love to stay here with you, but as you can see, I have other pressing matters to attend to. But, I will expect to continue this conversation once the operation is complete. We'll deal with the orb when we get back. For now, Donahue, stay with Wren. Take her to the infirmary, and I'll find someone else to look after Wren before you're deployed."

I wrinkled my nose, insulted that he thought I needed a babysitter, even though I was turning eighteen soon. However, this was not a battle I wanted to fight right now.

As Rob rushed out, I noticed Alex studying the orb. He'd barely heard Rob's instructions. Alarmed, I slammed the safe door closed, jolting Alex out of his trance.

Instinctively, I grabbed his arm, so he'd look at me. I shivered as his blue eyes shifted to my face.

I warned him, "Do not go near the orb. You have no idea what it can do…Or do you?"

Alex jerked his arm back, and I released my grip. "I told you I don't."

He quickly realized that his reaction alarmed me and apologized.

I explained, "I'm telling you that because I don't want you to get hurt."

He nodded slowly, realizing the seriousness in my voice. Shaking his head and looking around, he questioned, "Should I escort you to the infirmary now?"

DAIR's infirmary wing took up almost half of the floor. These doctors provided agents and employees with first-class care and recovery without having to go to the hospital in Ashborne. I assumed they had seen some unique and strange cases in the past. I had only been here once before, but my memory of that experience had grown hazy. This was where my robotics had been attached to my broken body nearly eight years ago.

This time, since my injuries were relatively minor, Alex led me into a small, stark-white room. The unmistakable odour of disinfectant wafted up to meet us as we entered. The few nondescript cots set up in the corner contrasted with the shiny high-tech machinery that lined the walls in odd, irregular shapes. An overwhelming number of buttons, levers, and screens were embedded into their sleek surfaces. I glanced to the side to see my blurry reflection staring back at me from the curved surface of a rounded, silvery-white contraption.

"Don't worry," Alex assured me, mistaking my curiosity for alarm. "Your wounds don't look that serious. Dr. Flores will have you patched up in no time."

I waved a hand at my surroundings. "What's all this for, exactly?"

"Well, that machine is for locating and extracting foreign, metal objects—like bullets—I believe. That's what those needle-thin scalpels are for."

Alex turned around and pointed out a large but flat rectangular machine. "That looks like it would be some kind of…uh…X-ray device." He squinted and leaned forward. "And that one…Could be a light source? It's probably very important."

Clearly, he had no idea what those machines were used for, and his uncertain smile made me laugh. I critiqued, "Do we really need all this stuff?"

"DAIR's advancements in technology have always attracted un-wanted attention. Some people would kill for it. DAWN—that stands for Designated Agents for the World's Needs, if you didn't know—any-way, its sole purpose is to keep people safe from dangers unknown to them," Alex told me as we walked over to a cot. "We risk our lives for the continuation of humankind, meaning we're going to get hurt, and it's better to be prepared for the worst. Besides, look at all this room we have. We can afford to fill it up with fancy machines."

I bit my bottom lip, wanting to change the subject. I had been one of those people who had suffered due to DAIR technology. Its first experimental time machine had caused a time storm, which resulted in my parents' deaths and my near-fatal injuries. I had mixed feelings about the technology developed here, even though the robotics designed by my uncle in this facility had saved me.

"DAWN's the security division of DAIR, right? Rob doesn't really talk about his work with me." Alex nodded, and I continued, "So, you do whatever it takes to limit the public's knowledge about advancing technology. For their own good."

Alex frowned, and his tone hardened. "It's a little more compli-cated than that. We protect humanity from deadly threats and immin-ent danger. We do what we have to do, and we do it well."

"In the future I travelled to, there was no DAWN or DAIR. No one to protect Ashborne and the world from a tyrant. Only you, Cass, and Tolli were there. It took you guys years to formulate and execute a plan to stop my future self."

He furrowed his brow as he tried to process my words. Curious, he asked, "Who's Cass?"

I wondered where Cass was. I narrowed my eyes, trying to sort out the two timelines I had lived through.

I explained to Alex, "Her name's Cassandra Viola, but you and Tolli called her 'Vee.' We were childhood friends. She lived down the street from my house, before my parents died. You haven't met her yet?"

"Nope. But I know who you're talking about. She's one of the new agents."

He turned away to greet the stout doctor with mocha-coloured skin who had appeared at the other end of the room. She pulled her hair back into a tight bun while she made her way toward us.

"Hello, I'm Dr. Flores. Let's take a look at you." The doctor's large, kind eyes studied the gash on my forehead and moved down to the multiple bruises and scrapes across my legs. I pulled my sleeve up to show her my arm. "Looks like you've been on quite an adventure, miss."

"I have," I replied as she gathered tools to extract the pieces of glass implanted in my skin.

The shock had fully worn off now, and I was starting to feel a sharp, throbbing pain in my arm.

As Dr. Flores dabbed the gash above my eye, Alex lingered close by for a little while before saying, "I don't think you need me for this. I can come back in about half an hour."

"Wait," I blurted, "please stay. I want to explain."

I weighed the consequences of revealing all the secrets I knew of an alternate future to him. I was desperate to lighten the heavy burden I carried, and my gut told me I had to trust him. In the future, we'd only had each other. I remembered the night up on the roof of the warehouse when his future self had told me that I could redeem myself. He wouldn't give up on me. If there was anyone in this alternate timeline whom I could trust with the information I held, Alex was that person. And I refused to give up on him either.

I held up the watch I had in my hand, and he paused before reaching out for it. He studied it, comparing it to the one on his wrist while I started jabbering away about my trip to the future. Eventually, he handed the watch back to me, and I slipped it on.

I told him everything I could think of about travelling through the threads of time with his future self, Tolli, and Cass. I described evil Wren taking over Ashborne and the bubble shield she created to protect the city that had ended up imprisoning it. It was difficult to explain the complex mission to stop her, but I did my best. I told him how encountering the physical orb I had brought into the future had been fatal for her, and she'd been banished from existence. The two of us couldn't exist in the same timeline. Unfortunately, the timeline was drastically affected by my actions, and the future had become unstable the moment I'd set foot in it. After evil Wren had been defeated, the timeline's disintegration accelerated. As we raced back to Tempus III, the entire reality began to collapse. I had barely made it out alive. Before the time machine brought me back, I'd handed the orb to the older version of Alex and watched him fade away into nothingness.

Alex nodded his head occasionally, but I could tell he was confused. I didn't blame him.

A shiver crawled up my spine when I described the orb and the impossible abilities it possessed. How had it ended up back in the safe? The laws of time travel or quantum physics shouldn't have allowed it.

While I spoke, I studied Alex's mysterious blue eyes. He seemed like the same person I had left behind in the broken shards of time. But I still had a gut feeling that something was off. I had more insight into who he was after spending time with him in the future, but, then again, he would now be walking down a completely different path. His eyes were evidence of a change, whether big or small was yet to be determined, but he didn't seem to be under the orb's influence. Perhaps I was just being overly paranoid. Maybe it was just an unexplainable ripple in the threads of time. Like the two watches existing together. Yet a part of me felt unsettled every time he looked at me.

Dr. Flores worked quietly. If she thought I needed more help than the superficial wounds she was treating, she didn't let on. As she finished stitching up the cut on my bicep, a familiar bulky figure with tangled, golden hair rushed in.

"Donahue! There you are! Mallick said I'd find ya here."

Dr. Flores smiled and left to clean up her supplies.

Tolli's pale-blue gaze fell on me and my robotics. My cheeks flushed with excitement to see my friend alive. His mouth broke into a playful grin, reflecting the personality of the man I had met from the future.

"No idea you had a girlfriend, buddy."

"We just met a few minutes ago," Alex answered curtly, clearly uncomfortable with that statement.

Tolli paused for a few seconds, then laughed awkwardly, "Uh…Is this a bad time?" His eyes darted back and forth between Alex and me.

I wanted to hug him. I wanted to both laugh and cry because he wasn't dying from a bullet wound and lying in a pool of his own blood. But, it was evident he didn't know me, so with great effort, I remained silent and looked away.

Oblivious to my thoughts, Alex inquired, "Why were you looking for me?"

"I noticed you were missing during our training exercise this afternoon." Tolli quickly closed his mouth when I turned back toward him.

"And?" Alex prompted.

"Uh…you know for that thing we gotta do later with those guys—"

Alex interrupted, "Wren knows a little of Aquarius Deep. Tolli, this is Wren Derecho."

Tolli held out his hand and clarified, "My name's Trevor, actually, but everyone calls me 'Tolli'…wait, Derecho? Are you related to William Derecho?"

I shook his hand and replied, "I'm actually his niece—was his niece."

"Oh. Right. I'm sorry." Tolli stared at me and slipped his hands into his pockets without saying anything more.

I smiled. "It's okay. You guys can keep talking about Aquarius Deep."

Tolli looked relieved and nodded his head. His tone shifted as he addressed Alex. "Okay, the reconnaissance team on the island just contacted the control centre. Everything is in place. Cyril doesn't suspect a thing! His machine is as good as ours."

"Wait, you guys are retrieving Whispers of Amelia? That's the main component of the third time machine," I exclaimed before I could stop myself.

Whispers of Amelia was the key to the third version of the time machine from the future—the only successful one. I realized this mission had higher stakes than either of them was aware of.

Tolli stared blankly at me, like I was speaking a foreign language. His lips parted slightly, but words escaped him.

"Yeah, I think that's what it's called," Alex answered for his friend. "A guy named Cyril Elton-Blackwood built it based on designs stolen from DAIR. We're not sure exactly what it does, but we know it's dangerous. The operation tonight will be to take back what's rightfully ours."

Tolli chipped in, "We've prepared for this mission for months. It's the biggest one we've had in a while."

"It'll go smoothly," Alex added. "We have nothing to worry about."

Tolli hesitated before replying with uncertainty. "We have to talk, though. Remember when you suggested..."

"I don't know. I can't talk about that now." Alex shot a glance at me. "And there are some other things I have to figure out first."

Alex pressed his lips together, a distant look in his eyes, while I wondered about the consequences of harnessing Amelia's power. Someone else could discover how to time travel and put us in an even bigger mess.

Alex turned back to Tolli and assured him, "We'll leave with everyone else. Don't worry."

Tolli seemed satisfied and lightly punched him in the arm. "Well, then, I'll see ya later, Donahue. Nice to meet you, Wren."

He stepped back and walked out the infirmary's door.

"Tolli's hair is even wilder than his future self's," I remarked, causing Alex to snicker but not reply.

I noticed he was rocking slightly on his heels and wringing his hands.

"You look worried."

"Oh, it's nothing," he shrugged. "In an organization full of secrets, paranoia is common. Tolli and I wanted to have a backup plan just in case, but it's better to leave things to Rob and Director Li. They're the best of the best. Maybe you'll get to watch the operation from the control room. I doubt Rob will be able to get you any more help today, but he'll want you close by."

He appeared reluctant to say anything more about Tolli's visit and gestured toward the exit. "I guess we're stuck together until I have to meet up with my team. Your robotics need a tune-up, anyway. Luckily, I can assist you with that. How about we do that first and talk to Rob after?"

I nodded and stood up. As we walked to the infirmary exit, I waved thanks to Dr. Flores, who was calibrating one of her many monitoring devices. She returned my wave with a smile and a nod.

I couldn't help but feel uneasy knowing this reality now had a completely different future. Changing the timeline hadn't felt like my choice, but in the end, I had believed it was the right thing to do. Now I wasn't so sure. On top of altering the future, time travelling had also unexpectedly affected the past. Alex's eyes were proof this timeline wasn't the same as the last one, and the orb's presence in this reality was truly baffling.

Why was it still here?

So far, it hadn't done anything but loom in the back of my mind. Waiting for something to go wrong was almost worse than the orb's taunting voice in my head.

But, there was something else I couldn't place my finger on. Perhaps I was paranoid too.

October 1, 2059, 8:30 pm...

I moved my metal fingers up and down, one at a time. The damaged parts of my robotics had stopped sparking randomly, and my metal joints no longer felt stiff. The batteries in the casing embedded in my metal wrist were now replaced with fresh ones.

I glanced around the workspace. After leaving the infirmary, we had made our way to this room which was stocked with tools, electrical parts, and power sources specifically used for mechanical repairs. A couple of DAIR scientists and an electrician in stained overalls quietly worked on the other side of the room, minding their own business.

It was hard not to compare my robotics to Alex's. He was the only other person I knew who had them. Mine travelled from my cheek and neck to my back and snaked down to my kneecaps. Like both my hands, his entire left hand had been replaced, but he also had leg braces that cut off at his ankles with fully replaced knees. Since Alex had worked closely with my uncle, he was quite familiar with his projects, robotics being one of them.

"That's much better," Alex remarked, his eyes scanning over my fingers.

The click of heels grew louder outside in the hallway, so we turned our attention to the opened door of the workshop.

To our surprise, the director of DAIR walked into view. She made eye contact with me as she walked past the door, and the clicking of her heels stopped abruptly. We stood up as she entered the room. She clutched a large TetraScreen in the crook of her arm and pressed her plump lips together. Not a hair on her head was out of place.

"Agent Donahue." She nodded in acknowledgement and turned to face me. "I don't believe we've been properly introduced. My name is Director Everlyn Li," she said in a business-like tone.

I grasped her outstretched hand and shook it.

"And I'm Wren Derecho, but you probably already knew that."

Director Li smiled curtly at me instead of responding, her demeanour cold and intimidating.

As she smoothed out the imaginary wrinkles on her blazer, she similarly addressed Alex, "Agent Donahue, Director Mallick needs to speak with you. Apparently, both of you are in the habit of not answering messages."

Alex apologized, keeping his eyes downcast. Director Li was not quite his height, even in her heels, but the authority in her voice more than made up the difference. "You should be keeping a TetraScreen on you at all times and responding appropriately."

Alex nodded as Director Li added, "Director Mallick is currently in the control centre."

She swivelled on her heels and started walking out. Alex glanced at me and motioned with a tip of his chin for me to follow her.

DAWN's control centre was located in a wing of the complex I had never been allowed to set foot in. I followed Alex and Director Li closely, taking in my surroundings. The area was filled with agents bustling about, typing on TetraScreens and speaking through silver and cobalt-blue earpieces. The agents' voices blended with sounds coming from high-tech computers, creating a low murmur.

DAWN's control centre was designed as a hub with screens and monitors covering every inch of the walls. The circular room was divided into sections for various agents who focused on communication, navigation, and surveillance. On one monitor, I could see the three-dimensional layout of an island with a multi-story building near the middle of it.

Rob stood in the centre, so he could easily address anyone at any given time. He was dressed in a dark-gray suit accented by a sleek, wine-coloured tie that was much more formal than the clothes he'd worn earlier. Currently, he faced the largest section of agents. They sat in front of a massive screen displaying a clearing in a forest landscape. The sun dipped behind it in radiant colours of pink, orange, and yellow.

Rob's attention was focused on his TetraScreen, but he was simultaneously listening to the reports of the agents surrounding him. When he finally glanced in our direction, his features softened.

Rob switched off his earpiece as he strode toward us and called out, "Donahue, I've been trying to reach you." Holding up a finger to ask us to wait for a minute, Rob spoke to Director Li as she approached him. "Director Li, the agents here are gathering up the last of their equipment. I have Agent Mercier double-checking that everything is in order, as per your request. The recon team is waiting in position."

With a slight nod of approval, Director Li left to talk to another agent.

Alex casually crossed his arms and inquired, "What do you need to see me about?"

Rob's gaze fell on me. "First of all, how are you feeling, Wren?"

"Still a little shaken…I don't know how or if I can fix what I altered…You believe me, right? I've told Alex everything and—"

Rob held up a hand to cut me off. "I'm really sorry. I can't get into that now. Aquarius Deep is active in three-and-a-half hours. Is the… object in the safe?"

"Yes, and Wren's room is locked," Alex answered for me. "I really think there might be something to her story. As crazy as it may sound, I don't think she just dreamt it up. Rob, our timeline could be in grave danger," Alex added as he nervously glanced at me, and then continued, "and I'm also pretty sure she doesn't want a babysitter. Uh, can I join the rest of the team now?"

Rob sighed, "Donahue, the reason I called you here is that I'm going to have to ask you to stay behind on this one."

"What?" Clearly upset, Alex protested, "I've prepped for Aquarius Deep for months. You need all the agents you can muster right now. You have no idea how important this mission is. All you need to do is listen to Wren—"

"Donahue, you need to stay here," Rob commanded and pulled Alex aside, so I wouldn't be able to hear their exchange.

Their conversation grew heated, but I couldn't make out the words as they spoke in angry whispers. Rob turned and started walking back toward me as if to signal he was finished with the discussion.

"I know you've been working hard to prepare for this mission," Rob said firmly, "but I have to go with my gut on this one."

"But—"

"I've made up my mind."

Alex gritted his teeth and clenched his fists. He persisted, "You're making a huge mistake!"

"That's enough, Donahue. You might say something you'll regret."

Alex's cheeks flushed, and he continued arguing, "What about 'Cover compromised.'? The message we received from the missing agents after they gave us the island's coordinates. What if a double agent is feeding Cyril intel? That could uproot the whole operation, and put the rest of our people in danger. At the very least, we need to come up with a contingency plan."

"We've been over this. It's not enough evidence to abort or re-role the entire mission. I have a team still searching for those agents. We've scouted Cyril's island base for two days, and Quan's infiltration is secure." Rob's expression didn't change. "I'm your commanding officer, and this is no longer up for debate. I have to make the best choice for you and our team."

"I can't let my friends down," Alex countered in a more desperate tone. "I can't let Tolli down!"

"You're sitting this one out. That's final." Rob turned and double-tapped his earpiece. "Confirm Agent Dean Irving is taking Donahue's place tonight."

Fuming, Alex pivoted on his heels and stomped out. I wasn't sure I should follow him.

"As for you, Wren," Rob turned back and pushed up his glasses, "get some rest. I'll meet with you first thing tomorrow. If anything else out of the ordinary happens, let me know and keep me updated."

I nodded, and he patted me gently on the shoulder. "And stick with Donahue for the rest of the evening. He'll cool down soon enough."

Rob turned to attend to the monitors as Director Li reappeared. I scurried out of the control centre to catch up to Alex.

2 HOURS and 48 MINUTES to TERMINUS TERRA

October 1, 2059, 10:42pm...

"The stealth crafts are heading out now," Alex spoke solemnly as he checked his watch. "I should be with my team."

He popped a blueberry in his mouth and slowly chewed.

Guilt gnawed at my stomach. I felt partially responsible he had been benched, and I didn't know what to say. Quietly, I stirred my cold, semi-solid chili.

I listened to the sound of him munching blueberries for a few minutes before he broke the silence, "How are you feeling now? I mean, both physically and mentally?"

I bit my bottom lip. "Physically, fine. Mentally, more stable."

"Less anxious?"

I nodded.

"I still can't wrap my head around how the orb got back into the safe," Alex said, rubbing his chin. "Wouldn't that be an anomaly in the space-time continuum?"

When I didn't reply, he sighed, "Let's talk about something else. I think we could both use a break." He thought for a moment. "How many years into the future did you say you travelled?"

His tone was lighter, and I could feel a smile tugging at the corner of my lips. "Eleven years."

"Hmmm, so that would make me about thirty and super mature. You have to tell me: What was I like in the future?"

"You were a jerk," I answered without thinking.

Amused, he chuckled, "Really? That doesn't sound like me."

"At first," I quickly added, my cheeks growing warm. "And that's because I tried to choke you…because you kidnapped me."

"Ah, well, I think that's fair, then," he quipped, nodding his head, which made his hair fall forward into his face.

I bit my lip before recalling, "You also hated it when I called you 'Donna.'"

He wrinkled his nose in disgust. "Understandably."

"It's because my future self called you that."

"Then you better not call me Donna if you don't want to turn into her," he warned jokingly, tilting his head.

Smiling, I continued, "Then you stopped hating me, and I stopped hating you, and we became friends. You were kind and caring and brilliant; I'll give you that. Your plan saved the future of our world."

He rested his chin on his fist, a concerned and serious expression on his face. "That's all great to hear, but you didn't really answer my question."

I raised an eyebrow. "What's that?"

"I asked you what I was like in the future. Like, did I gain the muscle mass that I've been working so hard on? Tell me I was completely ripped. Or—better yet—I grew a few inches?"

I burst out laughing as a wide, satisfied grin spread across his face. He polished off the rest of his blueberries and stood up. Just as I had finished clearing up my dishes, Rob entered the cafeteria.

"You *still* don't have a TetraScreen on you, Donahue?" he cautiously teased, but Alex hadn't quite forgiven him yet.

"What do you want, Rob?" he asked tersely.

Rob leaned against the side of the table. "I came to check on Wren to make sure she ate something. I can spare a few minutes while the agents are en route to Cyril's island."

I was happy to see him and sat back down. They followed suit.

I knew I didn't have much time with Rob, so I summarized what I had told Alex earlier. I finished my explanation with, "The whole reality crumbled apart, and everyone faded away into oblivion. I used a future version of Tempus II that Alex built using Cyril's machine, Whispers of Amelia, to come back to the present before it disintegrated too. On the way, I must have screwed up the timeline. I can't think of any other explanation for the alterations in this present reality. Alex's eyes aren't supposed to be blue, and the orb I had abandoned in the collapsed future is back in the safe."

Surprisingly, Rob remained stoic as he listened carefully to my story without interrupting. He stayed silent, deep in thought for what seemed like an eternity, before he finally sighed heavily, "You were right to want to build the time machine, Wren. I should have helped you earlier."

Furrowing my brow, I questioned, "What are you talking about?"

He clarified, "Well, I think you need to keep building your time machine."

"WHAT?!" I stared at Rob in disbelief, and my heart rate quickened.

"Uh, Rob, did we hear you right?" Alex asked, alarmed, before I cut him off.

"We're in this alternate timeline because of both the orb and Tempus! I thought things would be better, but they aren't. Who knows how badly I've screwed things up? How would a time machine be helpful right now?"

"Think about it," Rob encouraged. "Time travel was a last resort in the future. If things progress in this timeline like they did in the collapsed one, we might need a working time machine again."

My mouth went dry, and I slumped into my seat. I didn't like his logic, but I knew it made sense. Regardless, I couldn't accept it right now.

"If you were able to avoid an entire future with the power of the orb and Tempus," he reasoned, "it could be an enormous asset in helping keep our world safe."

Rob smiled to reassure me, but I only felt an all-consuming dread. The first excuse I could think of was, "Tempus II doesn't work."

Rob insisted, "I've seen your designs incorporating the orb into the time machine. It may not work now, but it will. I can help get you more funding. I mean, we could have Amelia in this building by tomorrow—"

"Wren, maybe you should get some rest before you think about this further," Alex interrupted urgently.

His voice jolted us back to reality, and we both realized he was trying to end the conversation before things escalated.

Rob's voice lowered, "Donahue's right. You're exhausted and overwhelmed. We can talk about this another day."

I rubbed my eyes with the backs of my metallic hands. "Sleeping would be very difficult at this point." My words wavered at the end and didn't sound as convincing as I hoped they would.

Rob's TetraScreen buzzed in his shirt pocket. He retrieved it and tapped his finger on the glass.

"Listen, I need to get back to the control centre." He hesitated before suggesting, "If you don't feel like sleeping, you two can watch in one of the observation areas. Our agents will touch down a few minutes before zero-one-hundred hours."

Alex shot a glance at me and asked, "What do you think? You could use the distraction."

51 MINUTES to TERMINUS TERRA

October 2, 2059, 12:39 am...

lex and I slipped back into the DAWN control centre, heading straight into one of the monitoring stations to watch the operation. Alex recognized a colleague, a man with a large, straight nose and dark features, among the small group of agents in the booth.

Alex headed toward him. "Saber, I haven't seen you in a while, man. How've you been?"

"Good morning, Agent Donahue," he replied with less enthusiasm.

"Well, I should say I haven't *heard* you in a while," Alex corrected himself and placed a hand on the back of Saber's chair. "I didn't think you were still in Communications."

Clearly irritated, Saber's eyes remained glued to his computer screen. "Same as always."

"Do you mind if we stick around? Wren here hasn't experienced watching an op unfold before."

Saber grunted and waved at a couple of chairs behind him. We took our seats, and I looked around the space as reports and updates from the deployed agents came through the main speaker. My eyes wandered to the largest monitor displaying a clearing in an area of dense vegetation.

"Where is that?" I inquired.

"All of the feeds are showing different areas on Cyril's island," Alex informed me and pointed to the largest monitor. "That exact spot is concealed from the watchtowers, which makes it ideal for landing the stealth crafts, specifically the Osprey. Even though they're equipped with invisibility cloaks, we don't want to take any chances."

I waited for him to finish before repeating, "Osprey?"

"Oh, yeah, the Osprey is our largest stealth craft, and the Sparrow is…well, it was lovingly nicknamed by the aviation techs for its size. I'll have to take you for a spin in the Sparrow sometime."

Foliage covered parts of the multiple camera feeds, but I could discern the shadowy figures of agents gathering.

"Half the feeds are from security cameras," Alex explained and casually folded his hands on his lap. "We hacked into their security system, thanks to Agent Kyler Quan, and now they're being looped on Cyril's monitors. The other views are broadcasted from the Osprey and the agents' body cams."

Saber grabbed a jet-black headset and started talking to someone on the other end. As he did this, a message came through the speaker beside him, "The recon team has made contact with the rest of the group, and the agents have been briefed. Agent Tolli reports they're waiting on Agent Quan."

Alex stiffened; I knew he wanted to talk to his friend. Saber sensed it too, even though he appeared to be fully absorbed in his work.

Saber pressed his lips together and waved Alex over. "You've got one minute, and I ain't doing this for you again."

"You're such a great friend," Alex teased as Saber handed him the headset and rolled his chair to the side.

"Tolli?"

The sound of Tolli's energetic voice through the side speaker brought a smile to my face. "Hey, Donahue! Good to hear from you! We're missin' you down here, man. Is everything okay on your end?"

Alex spoke into his mic, "It's all good here." It was easy to hear the frustration in his voice as he spoke to his friend. "How's the op going so far? Anything seem odd or out of place?"

"Nope," Tolli responded confidently. "Everything's goin' smoothly."

I looked up to see Rob staring at us. If he was annoyed, he didn't show it. He then turned and continued to converse with Director Li.

Muffled static rippled through the speaker before we heard another voice. "Quiet down! The whole island can hear you babbling…pathetic amateurs."

Alex wrinkled his nose in disgust. "Kyler Quan has arrived."

Tolli quipped, "Ah, you mean the world's most charming man. Even his hair is trying to get as far away from him as it can. Gotta go, dude."

Alex chuckled and placed the headset down before returning to sit next to me. Saber immediately rolled his chair back into his spot. The agents in the control room settled in to watch the events of Operation Aquarius Deep unfold.

Agent Quan was evidently the guy in charge. He ordered four senior agents to eliminate the security measures in the watchtowers. Alex pointed out Dean Irving, the large, muscular dark-skinned man who'd replaced him on the mission. Irving and a young woman with a blonde braid were sent off to scale the side of Cyril's stone building. They were tasked with transferring Amelia from the extraction point at the top of the dome to the Sparrow, which would be waiting nearby. Quan instructed a few agents to stay behind as the rest grabbed their necessary supplies and followed him into the dark night. I watched the monitors intently as Quan sent them off except for three agents, including Tolli. After throwing on matching guard uniforms, the four of them easily bypassed the security measures at the entrance on the ground level of the building.

Saber was now fully immersed in his work. I turned my attention away from the monitors to Alex and noticed him leaning on the edge of his seat. I shot him a worried look, so he nonchalantly leaned back and stretched his arms behind his head to cover up his anxiousness.

"Just wish I could have been there," he shrugged.

Nodding, I queried, "How does this end?"

"Best-case scenario: Cyril would be taken back to the DAIR compound, and Amelia would be secure. In the worst-case scenario…"

Before he could finish his thought, an irritating noise wailed throughout the room. We jumped up and hurried over to Saber as his thin fingers flew over the intricate control system.

Frantic reports echoed simultaneously around the room, "It's a trap! It's a trap."

"Tolli," Alex whispered, his blue eyes wide as he recognized his friend's voice among the panic.

Tolli's voice grew louder than the rest, "Donahue was right…something's off! Cyril knows we're here. Someone tipped them off! Backup…we need backup, ASAP!"

I winced as high-frequency squeals exploded out of the speaker. One last message came through from Quan, "Cyril's forces are overpowering us. Too late for backup. We can't win this fight. We're pulling out!"

Footsteps echoed in the background, and the sound of ricocheting bullets blasted through the speaker. Then it went silent.

"Sir," Saber shouted to Rob, "we've lost all communication."

As Rob barked orders to the people surrounding him, all the monitors started glitching, and then switched off simultaneously. Rob's voice stopped mid-sentence, and a deafening silence filled the control room. The eerie blue-green glow of the TetraScreens illuminated shocked faces.

Suddenly, a toneless voice shattered the silence, sending a wave of dread washing over the whole room. "Ah, Rob Mallick, I do hope you're listening."

Rob immediately regained his composure and hurried round the room to begin instructing his team to send reinforcements and re-establish communication. The clickety-clack of keyboards filled the room as DAWN personnel tried desperately to figure out what was happening.

Moments later, the monitors blinked on, one by one. Instead of the previous video feeds, however, the screens all showed the same footage of Cyril standing in front of a few blurry figures who were being restrained in the background. His machine, protected by a translucent magenta force field, stood at his side. I squinted and leaned forward as I recognized the large disc on top of a titanium box with levers, switches, and dials on the side. The metal disc, with eight metal talons protruding from the edges to the hole in the centre, sat on wide rubber tubing that connected it to the box.

My eyes darted from Whispers of Amelia to Cyril, who stood tall. He adjusted his striped tie and crossed his arms. The jagged scar on his face was not nearly as intimidating as his cold, piercing eyes.

Cyril continued, "You can't hide your secrets forever, DAIR. I've finally unlocked one of William Derecho's greatest accomplishments: an interdimensional transportation gateway. His work, however, was rudimentary compared to the advancements I've made. No need to applaud." He raised his hand in a mocking gesture, and then continued, "DAIR manufactures weapons of destruction, develops all sorts of advanced technologies, invents cures ahead of their time, and then locks away all their precious secrets until it benefits them. Why do you get to make these decisions? Who do you think you are?"

He gritted his teeth and smoothed back his long, black hair. "And, of course, when things go wrong, DAWN's always there to clean up the mess. No future can thrive in that system. It's all getting a little too old. Believe me, I would know."

Up to this point, I had been listening in a state of horrified shock, but at the mention of the future, my heart stopped, and fear beyond anything I had experienced before washed over my entire body. I was paralyzed with dread and couldn't move or speak, or even scream. All I could do was stare at Cyril's smug face on the screen.

A scuffle ensued behind him, but a team of guards quickly neutralized the threat.

Cyril raised an eyebrow at them. "Nobody is coming to save you fools…just like no one was there to help my daughter. Mallick, none of your pathetic DAWN agents will leave my island alive."

He turned his attention off-camera. "Becker, prepare my Amelia to be activated."

"Huh? Oh, right." A lanky scientist adjusted his oversized glasses as he slinked into the camera's range.

Cyril inhaled deeply, bowed his head, rubbed his eyes with his thumb and forefinger, and stayed silent for a few long seconds. When he lifted his head, the smirk on his lips was replaced with a quiver.

I could hear the depth of pain in his voice. "I watched my seven-year-old daughter die. DAIR could have saved her, but they refused. My wife abandoned me. I lost everything. You stole my whole world. Mallick. Li. Derecho. Every person in that cursed facility. Now, it's your turn."

I knew he was talking about Uncle William. Hearing my family name through the speakers made my stomach churn, but I still couldn't move. I could only listen.

The camera angle shifted to follow Cyril. Now we could see all the captured agents in the background. Cyril's men were no longer restraining them. Some were on their knees. Some were lying on their sides. I recognized Cass among them, her gray eyes burning with defiance, yet she remained silent. Sharp pain gripped my heart as I watched my childhood friend suffer, unable to do anything to help her. Tolli knelt beside her with a split lip, muttering something inaudible. Irving sported a swollen black eye and slumped on the ground, his eyelids flickering as he fought to stay conscious. The short, slender woman with the long blonde braid leaned against him. It was obvious she was holding back her tears as she tried to regain control of her emotions, but a few suppressed sobs made it through. Her body trembled as she surveyed the predicament of her teammates. The rest of the team was hardly visible in their black outfits.

Cyril addressed his guards, "Kill them."

"No!" I screamed, my voice returning.

Alex froze behind me with his fists clenched. I felt his shallow breathing on the back of my neck.

To our horror, the guards raised their guns to the back of the agents' heads and fired. Bullets collided with bone, and blood splattered across the bodies as they each fell to the floor.

My jaw hung open as tears blurred my vision. I had just spoken with Tolli a few hours ago, and now he was staring up at the sky with dull eyes, his body twisted unnaturally. I let out a sob as I watched him die a second time. Cass didn't even know I was alive before her skull was shattered.

I turned to Alex and collapsed. He caught me, but his eyes never left the screen.

Rob bellowed at the people around him to prepare for a full-armed assault on the fortress and sent agents scattering throughout the building.

He was disrupted by one last declaration from Cyril: "Amelia lives again."

The people left in the control room watched in horrified distress as he disabled the shield and activated his machine. Amelia produced an ear-splitting noise that tore through the speakers, causing us to clamp our hands over our ears. Helpless, we witnessed Amelia emit a beam of light from the hole in the centre of the clawed disc through an opening in the dome ceiling surrounded by glass panels.

Cyril had slipped on headgear to muffle the piercing squeal coming from deep within Amelia's mechanisms. The corner of his lips turned up, and his eyes blazed with a hollow joy. The camera feeds started glitching again, just as a shadow of fear passed over his face.

In the blink of an eye, a bolt of blinding white lightning blasted through the roof and struck Amelia, causing a gigantic explosion that funnelled upward.

The last thing we saw was Cyril and his guards flying through the air and hitting the floor. Cyril's eyelids were half-closed, and his once-groomed hair was a mess. A scarlet ribbon trickled from the wound where his scar had reopened. The faintest of smiles remained on his lips, reminiscent of his supposed victory.

The funnel cloud collapsed on itself, and the bodies disintegrated into a wave of energy.

≋ TERMINUS TERRA ACTIVATED

October 2, 2059, 1:30 am...

The massive blast shorted out the monitors with a series of electrical sparks. Shouts erupted throughout the control centre. Agents pecked feverishly on their TetraScreens and tried to connect the computers to a backup power source. Communications attempted to reach out to any remaining agents on the island to no avail. Soon, tremors under our feet increased by the minute, sending objects crashing to the ground. Smaller pieces of equipment fell from the walls. The floor wobbled and cracked, becoming more unstable by the minute.

"The foundations won't give out," Alex assured me, but his words sounded unconvincing as the quake shook the concrete beneath us.

I steadied myself against a wall as Alex stumbled into a glass partition. Sparks from the damaged equipment ignited small fires around the room. All the agents had jumped from their seats in alarm, but were hesitant to abandon their posts.

We heard yelling from just outside the control centre; someone was directing people down to the lower levels for safety. Rob and Director Li rushed around the room, still trying to establish contact with any of the surviving agents on the island. I doubted the island even existed if we were feeling the effects of the explosion hundreds of miles away.

TetraScreens beeped and vibrated as the rumbling intensified, adding to the assault on my eardrums.

"We have to get out of here," Alex said through clenched jaws.

People finally began to accept that all their efforts were hopeless and reluctantly joined the small crowd rushing out. Only Rob, Director Li, and a handful of agents remained.

Alex shouted at Rob, but his voice was drowned out by the cacophony of shattering glass and crumbling concrete. He grabbed my arm, and we steadied each other before fleeing toward the exit. I looked back at Rob. Sweat dripped down his face as he stood beside Director Li, who was furiously tapping on her large device, her lips pressed together in deep concentration. His expression shifted back and forth between grief, doubt, and persistence. On the way out, Alex snatched a cracked TetraScreen that had been left behind.

Before I knew what was happening, Alex pulled me away from the few stragglers rushing to the lower levels. The foundations moaned, creaked, and swayed. If the building collapsed, the best place to take cover was the underground bunker. However, Alex led me toward utility stairs at the end of the deserted corridor.

"What are you doing?!" I shouted, instinctively struggling against his robotic grip.

"We have to get to the roof!"

"WHAT?! Are you insane?"

He shot me a glance. His piercing blue eyes were full of determination, but I detected a hint of fear. "You have to trust me, Wren."

I took a deep breath and nodded. We flew up the flight of stairs, taking them two at a time. We were faster than the average person with the aid of our advanced robotics.

At the top of the staircase, we came across a hatch to the rooftop. In his haste, Alex ripped off the handle, warping the door. Luckily, it still opened enough for him to squeeze through. I followed him, pulling myself up through the gap into the cool midnight air.

Unnatural lightning struck sporadically in flashes of white and violet. Bursts of searing heat and freezing chills coursed through my body. As Alex tapped on his TetraScreen, I lifted my hand to my forehead to shield my eyes from the blinding bolts of light. In the distance, dark clouds rolled in from the horizon. Crackles of bright blue rippled through them, and I recognized what was coming. A time storm, large enough to spread from Cyril's island to the rest of the world, was unfurling in the sky.

"Something inside was jamming the signals," Alex explained, not wasting a second to even catch his breath. "I need to get this thing working, so I can find out the extent of the damage Amelia caused and if it can be fixed."

I peered over his shoulder at the device. Bright-red and orange masses rapidly spread across a grid emerging from Cyril's island, or where the island was supposed to be. Alex zoomed out to an image of the planet as the masses steadily consumed it.

My voice quivered. "Is that happening right now? Wha-what can we do? What's going to happen to us?"

Alex looked at me with defeat in his eyes, shaking his head. "My theory is when Cyril activated Amelia's portal, it created a time storm. Lightning from that storm collided with the beam of energy from Amelia, increasing the force of the reaction exponentially. The wave of energy from the explosion bonded with the time storm that had formed over the island, sending out expanding shock waves."

"What do you mean?"

"It means the whole world will self-combust in a matter of seconds…"

My heart pounded, throbbing throughout my whole body. I couldn't breathe as my throat constricted, and tears rolled down my face. Everything was happening so fast. My legs betrayed me, and I fell to my knees. Alex switched off the device and slumped down beside me.

This was my fault. It was all my fault.

"So, it's all over, then? I didn't stop anything. I only made things worse." I buried my face into my knees. "It's not supposed to end like this."

"Don't blame yourself. None of us could have known." Alex hesitated before wrapping an arm around my shoulders, his blue eyes glistening.

"There's really nothing we can do to stop it?"

Alex's shoulders slouched as he tossed the TetraScreen behind us. He clenched his fists, but didn't answer me.

TERMINUS TERRA COMPLETE

In my final moments, I recall the last words I had said to my future self in the alternate timeline.

"You chose this."

Her blue aura, radiating with supernatural power, had vanished.

She'd replied with fear in her emerald eyes.

"You chose this too."

I guess I did.

I'm dying.

I'm falling.

I'm flying.

The wind is at my back, and my limbs are flailing.

Glass-like shards surround me, defying gravity and refracting light.

I race through space, where a billion stars threaten to blind me.

I plummet through the vast and vibrant network of the threads of time.

Dark violet shadows rush past, seemingly tangible.

I've caught a glimpse of reality.

A fading glimpse of a time that never was.

It feels like I'm back in Tempus III, travelling to the present from a collapsed future.

But this time, I hit the floor of my room a lot harder.

PART TWO
ALEX DONAHUE

October 1, 2059, 3:43 pm...

Everything had exploded in brilliant light and colour as Wren disappeared. Blue. Purple. Then blue again. Closing my eyes did nothing to block out the overwhelming sensation. But before I could determine where I was, all of it vanished. I was enveloped in a suffocating, smothering void. I kicked my legs and flailed my arms, desperate to touch something...anything.

Just as sheer panic began to consume me, I was thrust out of the void and I collapsed to my knees. The clang of my leg braces hitting concrete echoed throughout the hallway. I took a few deep breaths as I brushed my thick hair out of my eyes. As I glanced up, I realized I was crouching in front of Wren's door.

Dazed, I looked over my shoulder to see a familiar figure standing behind me with his arms crossed and his round glasses perched on his nose. I froze, speechless, for a few long seconds. This had happened before. I had been here before.

I leapt up and choked out, "Rob...you're alive!" I looked down at my trembling hands, clenching and unclenching my fists. "I'm not dead? How did...why...Where are we?"

"Donahue, what are you talking about?" Rob questioned, his puzzled expression a mixture of concern and amusement as he tried to gauge whether I was playing a joke on him.

I patted my torso, remembering the wave of heat and pain that had ripped through my whole body. Still confused, I pinched the flesh of my forearm.

"I—I'm alive," I stuttered. "I don't…I don't understand…"

Rob's brow wrinkled. "Whoa, Donahue, slow down. What are you so confused about?"

"I don't know what's going on."

"Uh, well, I asked you to go grab some lock-picking tools, so we can get into this room to help Wren, the girl inside. Remember? I was worried about her, but now I'm starting to get a little worried about you."

I ran my fingers through my hair and wiped at the sweat collecting on my forehead. "I…what—What lock?"

I shook my head to clear the fog that clouded my brain, but it didn't help. My thoughts churned, and my stomach felt queasy.

What was happening to me?

Rob gestured to the door behind me. "That lock. Are you feeling okay, Donahue?"

I pushed up my sleeve to reveal the watch William Derecho had given me. It showed 3:47 pm. I thought of the inscription on the back, *'Aut viam inveniam aut faciam.'* The translation meant "I will either find a way or make one."

Was this another way to exist outside the laws of time?

"Donahue?"

I blinked hard, then bent over and leaned against the door to examine the lock. Without warning, it swung open, and I tumbled forward to the ground. I looked up to see a dishevelled and pale-faced Wren. Her eyes frantically darted around, landing first on me, and then on Rob.

At the sight of Rob, she cried, "What? Why—Alex—Why are we here? How are we here? Didn't we die? The explosion?!"

To my surprise, she rushed right past me to Rob, tears welling up in her emerald eyes. Unprepared for her aggressive hug, he stumbled back a few steps before catching his balance. As I picked myself up off the floor, Rob tried to comfort Wren.

Before Rob could say anything, I quickly asked, "Wren, we died, right? It happened. It was real, wasn't it? We were on the roof, we…"

Wren's head snapped up, and she let go of Rob. Her teary eyes filled with a sudden hope as she studied my face. "Yes, yes! You remember? It was real. It all happened!"

Relieved, I nodded and muttered, "But, how is this possible? We're back to 3:47 pm!"

"Wait," Rob interrupted, his face emanating confusion, "you two know each other?"

"Yes…well, sort of," Wren replied, rubbing her temples. "We met yesterday. Well…actually, we met yesterday again for the first time… um…"

"What? What are you talking about? You're not making any sense." Rob demanded, "What's all this about dying?"

Suddenly, Rob's bafflement turned to alarm as he noticed Wren's bandaged wounds. "Wren? What happened to your face?"

Gingerly, she touched the butterfly bandage taped above her eye. "It's okay, Rob. The doctor looked at it already."

"What? When? When did you see the doctor? You've been in your room this whole time!" Rob exclaimed.

Wren looked like she wanted to explain, and Rob leaned toward her. However, she stared at him with large eyes and remained silent with her lips slightly parted.

I put my hand on Rob's shoulder. "Rob, we have a lot to sort through. Can I ask Wren a few questions first to try to clear up some of the confusion?"

Rob's eyes narrowed in suspicion, but after a moment, his gaze softened and he nodded.

I turned to face Wren and suppressed the anxiousness growing in my stomach. I needed to stay calm. "What can you remember about the last few minutes?"

Wren, after realizing I had taken a deep breath to settle down, relaxed her shoulders. She closed her eyes and recalled, "I remember being on the roof with you, and then we were hit by the explosion's shock waves. I think I was in the threads of time, and I landed on the floor in my room. Then I heard you outside…"

Rob continued to stand in stunned silence as Wren trailed off.

"Rob, maybe we should go in the room for more privacy," I said, gesturing to the door.

He put his arm around Wren and guided her back inside to the closest chair.

Suddenly, he became aware of the disaster that was once Wren's room. "What happened to your room?"

"It's a long story, but I'm not hurt," Wren offered, gaining some of her composure.

"I have time. Can you please start at the beginning?" Despite his words, Rob glanced at the TetraScreen in his pocket.

Wren wrung her hands. "I think you might want to sit down, Rob. Something is very wrong with the timeline. I think we're living yesterday again."

Rob tilted his head and frowned. Both Wren and I knew there was no way we could fully catch him up right now. As she brushed her tangled hair from her face, Wren rose from her seat and approached the safe in the back of her room.

Rob's attention turned to the melted metal of the lock, but before he could say a word, we both interjected in unison, "It was a VU: a vaporizing unit."

I didn't think Rob could be any more confused than he already was, but I was mistaken. His mouth hung open, and he remained silent, waiting for us to continue.

I rubbed the back of my neck. "Is the orb still in there?"

Wren's lip twitched before she swung open the door.

There it was. The orb, glowing and mysterious and as alluring as ever.

Was it the reason for all of this?

To my understanding, the orb had been trying to control Wren.

Wren forced the safe door closed, warping the steel frame with her robotic strength. The sound of metal scraping against metal filled the quiet room, sending a shiver down my spine. She dusted off her hands and seemed satisfied for the moment.

As I gauged where we were in the timeline, I became aware that

Operation Aquarius Deep hadn't yet occurred. The realization triggered an immediate sense of urgency, and I knew I needed to warn Rob of the mission's impending doom. I could see Wren was also beginning to piece things together. As our eyes met, we silently agreed on what we needed to do next.

I turned to Rob and began to explain as best I could. "I know this is all sounding a bit crazy, but I think I've earned enough credibility with you over the past few years that you can trust me, even when the story seems a bit far-fetched. I know how it's going to sound, and I would react the same way you are if our roles were reversed. But, please listen to us. Something is very wrong with the timeline, and Wren and I need some time to figure things out. The problem is, we don't know how to explain what has happened to us."

I paused, thinking Rob would interrupt me, but he didn't. "We'll keep you updated, of course, but you really should be focusing on Aquarius Deep. My hunch was correct; there's a double agent. The whole thing's a trap. Cyril knows about our presence on the island and our plans for tonight."

"Okay. Who's the double agent?"

I hesitated. "Uh…I don't know that yet."

Rob clenched his jaw. "I appreciate your concern, Donahue, but we've been over this. There's no evidence. We've scouted Cyril's island base for two days, and Quan's infiltration is secure…" He turned to address Wren. "Wren, the orb—"

I cut him off aggressively, "Rob, you don't understand! Wren and I saw this mission fail once already. I know there's a traitor, and our agents are in grave danger! You need to listen to us!" I caught myself before I got too carried away. I could already see I wasn't getting through to him. I deemed it best to end the conversation and change the subject. "I'm happy to look after Wren until I get deployed, but I think she's fine."

Rob had patiently waited for me to finish before responding. "Donahue, I know you're worked up, and I'm surprised because this isn't like you. You know I trust you. However, I have a job to do, and I will do it to the best of my abilities. I can't change plans because someone has a hunch, even if it's yours. This mission has been finalized and approved by Director Li, and we'll do our best to make sure it's successful. I've heard your concerns, and I'll keep them in mind."

Rob glanced at Wren before finishing his previous thought. "Wren, you know how to handle the orb better than any of us. But, like we talked about earlier, I think we should bring it to people who specialize in otherworldly technology and alien power sources. They'll know what to do. I—"

Wren jumped in, her hands clenched at her sides, "I'm finished messing with the orb, and I'm finished with the time machine. You need to go back to work. It's very important that Aquarius Deep is successful."

Rob looked satisfied with her answer. He reached into his shirt pocket to retrieve his TetraScreen. Before he could contact anyone, he was interrupted by the director of DAIR. She appeared at the door in her expensive suit and navy-blue tie and knocked loudly to get our attention.

"Everlyn Li," Wren whispered.

Director Li narrowed her dark, almond-shaped eyes at Wren.

Rob jumped in, "Director Li?"

"I'm sorry for interrupting." She broke her gaze with Wren and turned toward Rob, frowning. "Director Mallick, we've been waiting for you in the control centre. Do you need to get your TetraScreen looked at? I don't think my messages are coming through."

Director Li adjusted her horn-rimmed glasses and left the room, without waiting for a reply.

Rob spun around, "You know Director Li?"

Wren opened her mouth to answer, but words escaped her.

He sighed, "I would love to stay here with you, but as you can see, I have other pressing matters to attend to. But, I will expect—"

"—to continue this conversation once the operation is complete," Wren finished, clasping her hands behind her.

Frustrated, Rob tightened his grip on the device and added, "We'll deal with the orb and everything that's going on here later. For now, Donahue, stay with Wren. Take her to the infirmary for a second opinion, and I'll find someone to watch her before you're deployed."

"I'm okay, Rob, but I'll do what you want," Wren told him as she gently turned him around and nudged him toward the door.

As soon as he exited the room, Wren and I turned to each other. She cupped her metal hands around her mouth.

"I'm definitely not okay. I screwed things up…I screwed everything up." Her eyes widened as she leaned on the wall for support. "What do we do?"

"I don't know."

"You're the guy who figured out how to time travel," she offered with a sliver of hope.

"Wren, I'm nineteen years old," I reasoned. "Time travel and time machines have only ever been a far-fetched theory to me until yesterday. I didn't even know you existed!"

"Technically, it's still today," she corrected.

I rolled my eyes. "Not helpful."

Wren tucked a piece of hair behind her ear and started to pace in a circle around her room.

She twisted her hair around her finger as she thought out loud. "First of all, why are we the only ones who are aware of this…this do-over? What sets us apart from everyone else?"

I shrugged, but the cogs in my mind had already started turning.

Wren continued, "We know Amelia must have had something to do with it. But, how would it decide where we start from? I wonder if it could only go back to when I restarted the timeline…"

"Yeah, possibly…I can't think of another explanation right now. How else could we have travelled back in time? I'm still stumped as to why it's just you and I who came back, though. Rob had no clue!"

She nodded, "Well, we're the only ones that we know of."

I repeated her questions. "So, what do we do? What *can* we do?"

Wren abruptly stopped pacing. "Aquarius Deep has to succeed. It's the only way to avoid another apocalypse. For some reason, we've been given a second chance to stabilize the timeline in this reality."

I rubbed my chin, deep in thought, and countered with, "Or we could go forward…to what time we're supposed to be in: tomorrow."

"How?"

Slowly, we both turned toward the metal hull of Tempus II. My gaze strayed to the safe.

"We could make it work. Break out of this place and go to the present…Or is it the future?" My voice trailed off before I added, "Otherwise, we could be stuck here. If we're not where we're supposed to be, that means that the timeline is already not working properly."

"No," she breathed out. "It would never work. I'd rather die than open that safe and operate that machine."

"Well, there's a chance you might," I half-joked.

Wren shot me a fierce glare as she swept her fingers along one of the time machine's sides.

"Too soon?"

She ignored me.

I wandered closer to the futuristic-looking machine. It had a long steel rod on the top, like an antenna, and round windows on the sides. Inside, I could see a control desk and one lonely seat bolted to the floor.

I chewed my lip. "Rob made a good point: there's a chance the time machine could solve all our problems."

Wren shook her head, her russet hair hitting her cheeks. "Tempus II's model is powered by the orb, and the last time it was turned on, it caused mass electrocution throughout the entire compound. Tempus III only worked because Amelia's metal disc was connected to it. We can't rely on building a time machine that may or may not work. We have to focus on stopping the apocalypse."

I raised my hands in surrender. "You're right. Time travel would only be a final resort. There are too many unknown consequences."

"So, how do we change DAWN's fate?"

"I had a hunch there was a double agent, and I was right. If we're going to do this your way, we need to expose the traitor," I pointed out. "We have a little less than eight hours until our team gets sent out from here." A fluttery feeling grew in my chest. "I have to go on the operation with Tolli and the rest of the team."

I shuddered, remembering Tolli's gruesome death. Tolli was the most trusted ally I had, and I'd watched Cyril's men blast a bullet through his skull. "Speaking of Tolli, we met up at the infirmary last time because that's where Rob told me to take you. Let's go find him."

We started walking down the bare halls in silence, the only sound coming from the echo of my boots on the concrete floor. As we turned a corner, I glanced at the butterfly bandage on Wren's forehead and the gauze pad peeking out of her collar.

"Did you get any more injuries from the explosion?"

She brushed her fingers across the bandage and assessed her robotics. In a relieved tone, she replied, "No. I think I got a few new bruises from falling through the threads of time again, but nothing serious."

"Good. We have some time to kill before Tolli meets us at the infirmary." I glanced down at my watch and suggested, "Maybe we should make a detour to the Division of Time Studies to check if there are abnormal energy signatures around the island. If Amelia's activation caused that massive of a time storm, there might be something there to help us to figure out what or why it happened."

≋ 8 HOURS and 5 MINUTES to TERMINUS TERRA

October 1, 2059, 5:25 pm...

After William Derecho's death two years ago, the funding for the Division of Time Studies (DTS) had declined drastically. However, DAIR had still seen value in it, so it was given a small corridor of the complex to continue its work. If there was something unusual around Cyril's island or an explanation for what happened to Wren and me, these people might have answers.

Wren and I slipped into a room where screens of various sizes flickered and hummed with constant activity. I noticed it was packed with instruments of all kinds stacked haphazardly in every available space. A few scientists milled about, their heads bent down to focus on TetraScreens and bulky research files. The sheer volume of intel that was streaming into such a cramped space was astounding. As we surveyed the room, our attention was drawn to a large screen displaying a world map with blinking red dots. Ominously, the label "ANOMALIES" was positioned above it.

A young scientist wearing a green polo shirt underneath his lab coat looked up and noticed us. He held a clipboard in one hand and a ceramic mug of coffee in the other. A maroon birthmark on his forehead was clearly visible due to his shaved head. As the man walked closer to us, I could see his plastic clearance ID tag read, "Paris Giles."

"Welcome to DTS," Giles said without enthusiasm. "Were you sent here to check on the anomaly readings?"

"Uh, yes," I lied. "Orders from Agent Mallick. Do you have any new information?"

"For the last few years, our main objective was to watch the activity inside the threads of time, track time storms, and record abnormal radiation signatures."

The scientist pointed at the map with his cup, then proceeded to take a sip, but ended up spilling coffee on his shirt. His face reddened as he swiped at the liquid, but he continued speaking. "The anomalies have increased in frequency by 3.1 percent in the last day, but haven't increased in threat level. I was just about to file a report."

I nodded, but didn't understand what he was saying. "And what exactly are these 'anomalies'?"

"We describe them as strange, unexplainable events happening around the world. We're monitoring and surveying them in case emergency measures need to be put in place." Giles's thin eyebrows knitted together. "They've been occurring now for about…eight years? I'm not sure when they started, but this is the only spike there's been since we began. Normally, the readings are quite low, so this is a little concerning."

"Right, right," I agreed and glanced at Wren. Her gaze flicked around rapidly as she studied the digital map. "Just to clarify, what kind of events are you talking about, and what are they being caused by?"

"Multiple strands in the threads of time—a dimension which holds the timeline and its secrets—have been affected by small, confined bursts of unidentified energy. We believe the result could be the timeline losing stability. We are currently monitoring these strange explosions. These are the most prevalent anomalies: our world time clock glitching and malfunctioning, growing activity in dormant volcanoes, sudden shifts in climate abnormal to the region, and slight tremors underground due to multiple tectonic plates shifting. However, these things aren't proving to be too threatening so far…other than being anomalies in nature, of course."

"How many of these explosions of energy in the threads of time have you identified?" I asked, running my metal fingers through my tangled hair.

"We've observed three so far," the bald scientist answered.

I gulped as dread rose in my throat. "The more recent anomalies aren't near the South Seas, are they?"

"Why, yes." Giles downed the last sip of coffee left in his cup and grimaced. I couldn't tell if it was because of the taste or the temperature. "Abnormal energy signatures are more concentrated around that area. How did you know?"

"Lucky guess." I shrugged, hoping he wouldn't pursue it further. I pulled Wren toward the exit. "Sorry, we really have to go."

⇛ 7 HOURS and 12 MINUTES to TERMINUS TERRA

October 1, 2059, 6:18 pm…

Wren and I strolled through the front doors of the infirmary and immediately recognized the physician standing at the other end of the room.

"Hello, I'm Dr. Flores," the stocky doctor called out as she attempted to smooth out the wrinkles in her blue scrubs.

Even though we had spent more time than we had planned at DTS, we were still a few minutes early to meet up with Tolli. Our discovery of the spike in anomalies was quite concerning, and the new information rolled around my mind as I tried to make sense of it.

Dr. Flores sauntered over, her eyes curiously darting between our silver robotics. "Do you need help with anything? Looks like you've been on quite an adventure, miss."

Wren nodded, feeling the butterfly bandage above her eye. "I—we—have."

Dr. Flores wrapped her dark hair into a bun and apologized, "I'm sorry, I don't recognize you. Were you treated here recently?"

Wren stuttered, "Umm…"

I jumped in to explain, "Wren's injuries have already been looked at, thank you. We're just here to meet a friend. He'll be here in a few minutes."

Dr. Flores's forehead crinkled, and she paused before answering.

"Okay. Well, it's a pleasure to meet you two. Feel free to wait out here, but I must get back to work."

As soon as she turned around and slipped into the next room, Wren asked me, "When is he supposed to get here?"

I checked my watch for what felt like the hundredth time in the past couple of hours. "Any minute now."

"How much are you going to tell him?" Wren questioned and then whispered, "Are you going to tell him about what'll happen if Aquarius Deep fails?"

I hesitated and tried to suppress the memories instantly flooding my mind. "We won't fail this time. We already know what happens, so we're one step ahead." I pressed my lips together, then added firmly, "I won't let them die again."

Unfortunately, the words I spoke served more as empty bravado than strong conviction. Wren's gaze fell to the floor, and her silence betrayed her doubt.

For a moment, a twinge of fear rose in the pit of my stomach; however, I pushed it down and continued talking, "I think I'll only tell him about the double agent. There's no point in confusing him with things we can't figure out right now. Remember how confused Rob was even after we explained our situation the best we could? I want to tell Tolli everything, but I don't think it'll be beneficial."

Instinctively, I glanced over my shoulder to see if anyone was within earshot. Wren still didn't reply. In the silence that followed, I couldn't help but recall the lifeless faces of my friends slumped to the ground among splatters of dark blood. The image of Tolli's dull eyes staring at the sky sent a sharp pain through my chest.

Suddenly, Tolli walked in behind us and startled me, "Donahue! There you are! Mallick said I'd find ya here."

I swivelled on my heels to see my closest friend alive and as charismatic as ever. Overwhelming emotions caught me off guard as I was greeted by his familiar lopsided grin.

He stopped in his tracks after noticing Wren, and his mouth widened even more. "Huh, no idea you had a girlfriend, buddy. Is this a bad time?"

"No," I choked out.

Impulsively, I embraced Tolli, surprising us both. He tilted his head in confusion, his arms stuck at his sides.

"Donahue, what's gotten into you?" Tolli's cheeks reddened. His gaze darted from me to Wren. "Uh, just so you know, we don't usually hug every time we see each other."

Wren had also been affected by the sight of Tolli as her entire demeanour brightened. She simply laughed and looked away as tears welled up in her eyes.

I released Tolli in slight embarrassment and gave him a hearty slap on the back, blinking hard. "Missed you. That's all."

"Uh...okay." Puzzled, Tolli took a second to think before remembering why he had been looking for me. "I noticed you were missing during our training exercise this afternoon...uh...you know for that thing we gotta do later with those guys..."

He threw Wren a sideways glance, but she reassured him. "Tolli, I'm aware of Operation Aquarius Deep."

Tolli squinted his pale-blue eyes at Wren. "How do you know my name? Is this a prank? Is that why Donahue hugged me?"

"No, I was just telling her all about my bestest friend in the world," I said in a sarcastic tone to change the subject.

"Okay..." Tolli shrugged and continued, "Anyway, the reconnaissance team on the island just contacted the control centre. Everything is in place. Cyril doesn't suspect a thing! His machine is—"

"Yeah, we know, Tolli." I placed my hand on his back and started guiding him toward the infirmary's exit. "Let's go. Come on, Wren."

"Dude, you're being really weird." Tolli laughed awkwardly. He called over his shoulder to Wren as she followed us out into the hallway, "Your name is Wren? Like the bird? My name's Trevor, actually, but everyone calls me 'Tolli.'"

Scratching the back of his head through his mess of blonde hair, he turned to me and added, "Oh, and Mallick is sending Irving with us on the Sparrow. Have you met him yet? He was added to the op at the last minute. I guess you could say I'll be mentoring the both of you since I have seniority."

I raised an eyebrow at him. "Seniority…by, like, six months."

He shrugged. "Six months longer than you."

"Seniority doesn't equal maturity, Tolli."

Wren had followed closely behind as Tolli and I entered DAWN's impressive weapons vault. Numerous agents were systematically going through various preparations for the upcoming mission. Some clustered around a senior agent to review coordinates on several maps while others cleaned equipment and loaded weapons into small crates. A few agents noticed Wren, but didn't pay her any attention. As Tolli left to change into his combat gear, Wren and I stayed off to the side, near a rack of laser tasers.

"I'm coming with you," Wren whispered, aware of the nervous energy that filled the room.

"Absolutely not," I responded as I slipped a laser taser into my tactical belt. "There's no way Rob would allow you on a DAWN op without any prior training. And what kind of person would I be if I put you in danger? Absolutely not," I repeated. "End of discussion."

My imagination went into overdrive as I thought of all the ways she could get seriously hurt. As much as I didn't want to leave Wren behind, she was inexperienced and untrained. I knew her robotically-enhanced strength and agility set her apart from the average person, but she would still be an extreme liability.

"I've travelled to the future and helped you save the world," she persisted, surveying the laser tasers. "That has to count for something. I'm not going to just wait here while you change the fate of the world by yourself."

"This is the present reality, not the future," I countered. "You've seen firsthand what Cyril is capable of…how ruthless he can be. His guards will kill you on sight. You're not going anywhere near that island."

Her voice quivered, and her eyes glazed over with angry tears. "I just watched two people I cared about die in the other timeline, and now I have a chance to change that. Please, let me help. Let me do something. Anything!"

I sighed, impressed by her courage, but frustrated by her stubbornness. I placed a magnetic, disc-shaped explosive against the inside of my metal wrist. The force of the tiny magnet held it conveniently in place and made it readily accessible when needed.

I continued more gently, "Wren, you'll never get authorization from Rob. I need you here, close to him, in case things go south, and you need to explain everything to him. It would be easier for you to spot any suspicious activity from the control room. You can help me find the traitor that way. Also, if the anomalies increase exponentially, I need you to let me know right away. Only the two of us are aware of all this, so we can't afford to make our decisions lightly."

She held my gaze for a second before glancing away. "Fine."

"What's wrong?"

"Nothing…I don't know…I'm still not used to your eyes."

I had forgotten she'd been in an alternate reality, and I fumbled for words to reassure her. "If it makes you feel any better, I've never used the orb or even touched it. William only showed it to me once, years ago. Actually, it was on the day he died," I exhaled heavily. "I'm sorry, I didn't mean to…I think I'm making it worse…"

She bit her lip and crossed her arms. I knew I had to make things right between us.

"Wren, you're one of the bravest, most intelligent people I've ever met, but we may not get another chance to right our wrongs. Do you trust me?"

She remained silent for a moment, processing my words. With a tinge of disappointment, she nodded. "All right. It's okay, Alex. I do trust you."

"I'll be in contact," I assured her as I walked over to a nearby bench and sat down. I motioned for her to sit beside me, deciding it was best to change the subject. "You told me what I was like in the future. What about Agent Viola and Tolli?"

"Agent Viola? Oh, you mean Cass. Well, I've known her since I was little, but we lost touch after my accident. I didn't even recognize her when I saw her again, but she definitely knew who I was. She was...different from what I remembered." Wren avoided looking at me and smoothed out her shirt. "Colder. Standoffish. Like she carried a lot of emotional baggage. I...I think her life had been pretty hard. But, even so, within a few hours of spending time with her, I remembered how much she meant to me. I hope she felt the same way."

"Well, she certainly has that reputation around here. I don't think anyone would want to get on her bad side. Maybe that's why I'm not too eager to meet her." I laughed.

"Hey, that comes in handy sometimes," Wren pointed out. "She's had to stand up for herself."

"So, she's a bit rough around the edges. I think that's kinda normal around here."

"Maybe, but that girl is scary-rough. I don't know if it's normal to be able to fight like that. And don't flirt with her either," she suggested, shaking her head and giggling, "or she'll sucker-punch you in the stomach. Tolli's brother found that out the hard way."

"Really? Noted. Wait, how did you meet Aaron—"

"He has a garage in Ashborne. Or will have one. We needed his help."

"Wow. Tolli has an...interesting background." I thought back to the things Tolli had told me about his family. It had always sounded like he never wanted to see them again. I added, "I've learned it's best not to bring it up. We must have been desperate for him to go to Aaron for help."

"We were." Wren smiled and motioned behind us. "Anyway, the only person who could tease Cass and get away with it was Tolli. I guess he just wore her down."

As I met Wren's gaze and chuckled, I realized I'd never quite met anyone like her. She had experienced so much trauma in her life, but it didn't seem to have dampened her fiery spirit. In fact, it seemed she had come out of it with more courage and appreciation for life than before.

"And Tolli was..." Wren suddenly shut her eyes and tensed up, gritting her teeth. Before I could ask what was wrong, she swallowed hard. "Sorry...just reminded of something."

Tears sprang to her eyes, but she suppressed whatever she was feeling and continued, "Tolli was the nicest to me. He made me laugh whenever I wanted to cry. And he was so loyal to his friends. It's no surprise everyone likes having him around." She joked, "But he was also really bad at explaining things. Like time travel."

As if he knew he was being talked about, Tolli wandered over, laser taser in hand. "Ready, partner?"

I jumped up and whisked around to retrieve a silver and deep-blue earpiece from a row of foam casings. I double-tapped it and programmed it to only sync with the one planted in my ear.

"Double-tap it to switch it on and off. Hold to talk." I demonstrated before placing it in Wren's hand with an encouraging smile. "Use it for emergencies and updates. No one's gonna get killed on my watch."

October 1, 2059, 11:58 pm...

Tolli and I headed into the DAWN hanger after walking Wren to the control centre. I felt better knowing she was safe with Rob and Director Li.

We arrived to see the tail of the Osprey disappear out of the hanger and toward the runway. The Sparrow, silver and black with a rising sun insignia on the side, stood in front of us. It was much sleeker and more aerodynamic in shape than the Osprey, and it was less than half the size at a length of fifty feet, with a wingspan of thirty-two feet.

Each aircraft served a different purpose. The Osprey had three armament stations positioned on the sides and belly of the aircraft, ready for aerial warfare. It was more than one hundred feet long, with a wingspan of seventy feet. It was also equipped with DAWN's top-secret Intelligent Weapons System (IWS) that made it one of the most formidable aircraft in the skies. Part of IWS included a cloaking system that could render the Osprey completely invisible, both to the naked eye and the most advanced radar systems. It was meant to carry twenty to twenty-five agents in style and comfort.

In comparison, the Sparrow was built for a much smaller crew. It was fast and quiet, with a hydrogen-fuelled engine, better for ops requiring maximum stealth. It was also equipped with IWS and had incredible agility when it glided through the air. I preferred the Sparrow as it could reach speeds of Mach 7, although Tolli and I got in trouble with Rob the time we discovered that.

As we circled around the Sparrow, we found Dean Irving, one of the new recruits, leaning his large frame against the side. He grinned at us, and I noticed some of his teeth were missing. His muscles rippled and strained beneath his tight black shirt with each movement.

As we approached, Tolli looked up and acknowledged him with a nod. "Irving."

It was unusual for another guy to make Tolli look so small. "Hey, Tolli!"

I also looked up at Irving. "So, you're the rookie."

He met my gaze, his eyes bright with excitement. "It's Agent Donahue, right? Part-man, part-robot?" His eyes locked onto my left hand, the only visible part that gave me away. "You're shorter than I thought you'd be."

I didn't answer and pushed past him to climb through the aircraft hatch.

I heard Tolli pat the Sparrow's metal hull and say, "Good to see you, little lady," which immediately lightened my mood.

If everything went according to plan, and I survived this flight with Irving, we would arrive on Cyril's island a little before zero-one-hundred hours.

The flight time consisted of a few short conversations, mostly between Irving and Tolli. Tolli piloted the Sparrow, and I sat next to him. Irving was seated behind us in the jump seat that folded down from the starboard side. Even in our stressful situation, it was still entertaining to see such a large man try to sit comfortably on such a small seat. However, I was careful not to let my amusement show. I could easily imagine Irving squashing me like a bug.

I glanced around the cockpit at all the computerized windows. They were transparent and programmed to display three-dimensional images. A model of the island and the layout of Cyril's fortress were projected from multiple angles. My gaze was drawn to the image of the clearing, where all the agents would assemble before moving out.

Rob's voice was clear and his instructions concise as we listened to him review the specifics of the plan through the cockpit speaker for the third time today. He finished by emphasizing the goal of the operation, "Your mission is to retrieve the machine and bring it to me."

An image popped up on the centre window, displaying Whispers of Amelia. According to Wren, the metal disc sitting on top of the wide but short rubber tubing was the key to time travel.

"What the…" Tolli muttered, his attention shifting to Amelia's image.

Irving got up and leaned on the back of our seats, bending them forward under the strain. He reached out and used his thick index finger to zoom in to the titanium control box and view a computer-generated cross-section of the inside. It contained a liquid battery with a jumble of wires connecting it to the disc and the controls. The scientific part of my brain immediately wanted to dissect the machine to see how it worked.

Rob's voice interrupted our thoughts. "Cyril Elton-Blackwood created this machine. He's a tech genius who can hack into anything, and he managed to hack his way into one of DAIR's protected files and based his machine off William's old design: one that never received clearance to be built. That's what we're worried about. We have no idea what Cyril's machine can do."

I shuddered. I knew all too well.

"Please stick to the plan, and don't do anything stupid," Rob concluded.

"Roger," I said as I turned down the speaker.

I knew Rob had directed his last statement to me. This op had been planned for months, and I wanted to believe everything would go perfectly, but it didn't feel right to ignore my hunch. That could cost the lives of my friends and the mission. However, disobeying orders also had huge consequences. If I was going to identify the traitor and stop

Cyril from activating Amelia, I had better find a way to do it while still following orders.

As we neared our destination, I switched on the Sparrow's invisibility setting to blend into the night sky. The cloaking device reflected our surroundings, hiding the stealth craft in plain sight.

Tolli rubbed his chin before asking, "Are we gonna stick to the plan, Donahue?"

Irving piped in from the back, "What do you mean?"

"Nothing," I snapped. "We need to be alert; that's all. I suspect we have a traitor in our midst, but I have no proof. I just want the mission to run as smoothly as possible. Rob knows what he's doing, and the control centre has our backs. For now, keep your guard up, and if anything seems suspicious, speak up."

We approached the island, and Tolli guided the Sparrow toward a clearing in the thick vegetation. We rolled a few feet forward on the uneven terrain before stopping with a jolt. The three of us unbuckled our seat belts, put on our night-vision goggles, and armed ourselves with weapons from the compartments in the back. One by one, we jumped through the hatch at the bottom of the aircraft, plunging into the moonless island night. Only a few twinkling stars were visible in the darkness.

We jogged a quarter mile to meet up with the rest of the team assembling near the Osprey. Some agents were busy unloading crates while four senior agents checked over the equipment. These guys were the most experienced and longest-serving agents on the team, earning them the respected nickname "the Vets."

A slender, fierce-looking woman with olive-toned skin and a jet-black bob strolled over to us. Even though she was a part of the recon team that had already been on the island for two days, she still managed to look stunning. Wren had called her Cass and told me she was an elite fighter in hand-to-hand combat; however, I had already heard about her skillful dominance in the last round of recruitment trials nine months ago. Word had spread quickly because her abilities had impressed even the higher-ups. Only four agents, Irving and Viola being two of them, had been accepted and went through vigorous and demanding training before graduating from their probation period.

"Oh, hey, Vee. How's island life goin'?" Tolli called out.

"Not too bad." Her steel-gray gaze wandered to me.

"My name's Donahue. I don't believe we've met," I said awkwardly, feeling slightly intimidated by her striking physical appearance.

"I'm Vee." Her lips lifted into a half-smile. "And I know who you are. I've read your DAWN file."

Agent Adeline Jessie suddenly appeared beside her. Her pale cheeks were smeared with camouflage paint. A few leaves and twigs were tangled in her long blonde braid. "We're just waiting on Quan."

Vee rolled her eyes. "Quan's always ticked off if he has to wait for anyone. He was supposed to be here already."

"I'd be careful if I were you. He's already not happy about you being assigned to this op," Jessie warned. She quickly explained to the rest of us, "During our final assessment in February, Vee shot Quan with a ghost blaster."

Vee placed a hand on her hip. "And he's hated my guts ever since."

Tolli snickered, "I remember. Best day ever."

"Looks like it's you and me, Irving," Jessie piped in. "Hope you know how to use a grappling hook."

"Awesome." Irving held up his hand for a high-five purposely just out of her reach and teased back, "What's a grappling hook?"

Jessie responded with, "Team Jerving!" and jumped as if to take the challenge of his upraised hand, but countered with a playful punch to his exposed midsection.

"Oof," said Irving, holding his gut.

Still laughing, Jessie handed Vee a white rectangular device the size of her palm. "Oh, Vee, look what I found on the Osprey."

Vee held it up and examined it. On one side of it, there were varying shades of gray buttons and tiny grills of metal protruding on the end.

She stroked the surface with her thumb. "What is it, Addy?"

"I dubbed it the 'Circuit Toaster' because it disrupts strong electrical currents. I think it's for emergency shutdowns or something...

anyway, I thought it might be useful," Jessie replied and shrugged. "You may need it."

A wiry figure emerged from the dense vegetation on the edge of the clearing and shouted, "Quiet down! The whole island can hear you...pathetic amateurs."

Kyler Quan walked toward us, a gray and brown backpack slung over one shoulder and his signature mohawk standing tall. He removed one of his earpieces that had connected him to Cyril's security team and shoved it into his pocket.

Vee straightened up and announced, "Agent Quan has joined the party."

Tolli joked, "Ah, you mean the world's most charming man. Even his hair is trying to get as far away from him as it can."

This time I didn't laugh with the rest of my friends. Pressing my earpiece and adjusting the setting, I switched the link to speak to Wren, "Kyler's here."

"Be careful," she answered. "The anomalies are growing slightly, but not beyond what was predicted. Nothing looks off."

"Copy that."

"Irving, Jessie, with me!" Kyler yelled, marching over to the other group of agents to start giving orders.

The Vets tasked with securing the four outer watchtowers disappeared into the forest while Irving and Jessie ran to grab harnesses and grappling guns from a crate next to the Osprey. Rob had them assigned to scale the building and prepare Amelia's exit route to the Sparrow. The two of them gave Kyler a quick salute as they raced away, and the huge duffle bag strapped across Irving's chest didn't slow him down for a second. Agent Bree O'Connor, recognizable from her shock of ginger curls, and another agent remained with the stealth crafts under orders to have them ready to fly at any given moment.

Kyler hissed at us, "I could hear you guys on the comms. We're on a mission, and you guys are busy nicknaming something?"

"Well, we don't have to call it that," Tolli retorted under his breath.

"You don't need that thing; I'm completely capable of disabling

Amelia's shield without it." He held out his hand to Vee. "Give it to me, Viola."

Vee reluctantly complied, and Kyler pocketed the device.

"Unfortunately, I will be stuck with you three tonight." Kyler smoothed the side of his stiff mohawk and trudged past us toward the edge of the clearing.

We followed him without a word.

After he had returned his other earpiece to his left ear and blended into the brush, he added sarcastically, "Try to keep up."

31 MINUTES
to TERMINUS TERRA

October 2, 2059, 12:59 am...

O ur boots trampled the undergrowth, our steps in sync with the steady rhythm of our breathing. As the watchtowers came into view, the starry sky expanded, and the dense vegetation thinned out. It was bright enough for us to remove our night-vision goggles. Kyler stopped and dug into his backpack to pull out three guard uniforms identical to his navy-blue and black one. We hurried to slip them on, and Vee and Tolli tucked their hair into their peaked caps. Vee's top hung a little loose, and Tolli's was a size too small.

Tolli whispered, "Can I exchange this for a larger size?"

Even Kyler couldn't help but crack a smile. "Sorry, dude." I heard his voice echo through my linked earpiece. "Stand by..."

As soon as we saw a lone guard enter the building, Kyler gave the signal. The watchtower ambush was set in motion.

I crouched silently beside Kyler, Vee, and Tolli until Saber, back at Communications, confirmed, "The watchtowers are secure. Proceed."

"We're up," Kyler announced. "Heading to the entrance now."

I shoved my metallic left hand into my pants pocket as the four of us casually entered the stone building. Anyone who happened to look our way didn't pay much attention as they recognized Kyler as Cyril's head of security.

"We're in," Kyler reported through his earpiece.

We made our way through the first floor toward the elevator on the far side, bypassing a handful of bored-looking guards as well as some bustling scientists in billowing lab coats.

As we entered the elevator, I noticed some guards about to march by, and I saw my chance to separate from my team. Before the doors closed completely, I slipped out and joined the crowd. Tolli, Vee, and Kyler looked surprised, but they couldn't react.

I mumbled a quick explanation into my earpiece after I broke away from the group of guards. "I want to secure the stairwell. Meet you guys at the top."

I switched off my earpiece and started climbing the stairs closest to the elevator doors. This gave me a few moments to talk to Wren. Keeping my head down, out of view of any security cameras, I adjusted my earpiece's settings and turned it on again.

"Wren, are you there?"

"Yes. What happened?"

"I needed to get away from my team. If I'm stuck with everyone else, I won't be able to do much if we all get captured. Does anyone look suspicious to you at all?"

"No."

I leapt up the stairs as fast as I could. "Can you see a layout of the building on one of the screens in front of you? They must have some sort of control centre in this place to launch a digital attack on a communications system as sophisticated as DAWN's."

There was a pause before she answered, "Yeah, you're right. There has to be one, but I can't see anything here that would help you find it."

I nodded as my heart pounded with each step I took. My inner clock told me we had very little time before our communications would be cut off.

"Okay, Wren, I'm almost on the top floor. Tell Rob the rest of the team needs to be ready to storm Amelia's room now. I'll create a diversion; that'll be their signal to attack."

"How are they going to know what the signal is?"

"Don't worry," I assured her, "They'll know."

I switched my earpiece back to the original setting, wincing as Kyler's voice burst through, "—you hear me, Donahue?!"

"Right behind you. Stairwell is secure, boss," I replied nonchalantly.

Kyler's rant was interrupted by reports from the rest of the team. Vee whispered, "Jerving, are you in position?"

Along with a ripple of static, Jessie breathed heavily, "Nearly there."

O'Connor added, "The Sparrow is in position."

As soon as I made it to the top floor, my earpiece exploded with panicked voices.

"It's a trap!"

"Fall back!"

"Send backup!"

"Cyril knows we're here. I repeat—"

Beads of sweat collected across my forehead as I recognized the same chaotic shouts from the last timeline. I squeezed my eyes shut and clenched my jaw, trying to block out resurfacing trauma. I took a few deep breaths to calm my racing pulse and tried to contact Wren again, but all our comms were down. I glanced at my watch and figured I had about fifteen minutes to stop Amelia from destroying the planet.

Cyril's voice rang throughout the top floor, "Ah, Rob Mallick, I do hope you're listening."

I checked to see that I still had the small pistol from the stealth craft I'd tucked into my boot. I clasped it inside my left pocket as I strode over to the opened doors. I nodded at the guard standing stone-still outside the entrance as he held his rifle diagonally in front of his body. He ignored me, so I continued to walk through the thick metal door frame into a large, circular area. Immediately, I saw Amelia under a pink shield in the centre of the room.

I made sure no one was watching and took the tiny disc-shaped X-82 explosive, known for its concentrated blast, off my wrist and brushed my hand against the nearest metal shelf. The bomb attached itself and let out a small beep as it activated the remote-control signal. I reached inside my pocket and palmed the small fob that controlled it, making sure the red light was blinking.

It wasn't too difficult to blend in with the other guards as long as I kept my head down and stayed in the shadows. I walked to the right, along the curved concrete wall, keeping my pace slow as to not cause suspicion. I was thankful for the various pieces of bulky equipment stacked on high shelves scattered on the outskirts of the room that provided some concealment. As I joined the small group of guards surrounding the captured DAWN agents, I caught a glimpse of Cyril's stocky frame near Amelia. He had his back to me as he addressed the camera in front of him. The gangly scientist, Becker, stood off to his left, directly in front of Amelia.

Cyril began his speech, "You can't hide your secrets forever, DAIR. I've finally unlocked one of William Derecho's greatest accomplishments: an interdimensional transportation gateway. His work, however, was rudimentary compared to the advancements I've made. No need to applaud." He paused to raise his hand for a moment.

I stepped closer toward the middle of the room, still staying with the group of guards. I now had a straight path to Cyril and could see him more clearly. I could also see Tolli's face. A large swollen bruise had formed on his cheek, and blood dripped from the split in his lip. He looked up and noticed me, and I winked at him. Hope shone in his pale-blue eyes.

Cyril's accusations pulled me back to reality. "…Why do you get to make these decisions? Who do you think you are?"

Out of the corner of my eye, I caught sight of someone running into the room and glanced over my shoulder. His coal-black mohawk was unmistakable. I froze.

Kyler Quan, bent over to catch his breath, straightened up, and announced, "We have one agent not accounted for somewhere in the building."

My heart dropped as I realized he had not been executed with the others on camera the last time. Our gazes locked as I stared at DAWN's traitor.

I had a split-second to act. Without hesitation, I pushed the button, and the small but powerful blast of the X-82 echoed through the room. It all happened so fast that Kyler didn't have time to react before shrapnel tore through his body. In one fluid motion, I tossed the fob, spun around, and made a beeline for Cyril. I tackled him to the floor as he stared in stunned disbelief. That was all my team needed to take their captors by surprise.

The room erupted into chaos as DAWN fought to turn the tide of fate. As if on cue, four of our agents crashed through the glass panels in the dome ceiling and rappelled from the roof. They fired their weapons as they descended on Cyril's guards and entered the fray.

As I fumbled for my pistol, Cyril reached up to shove me off. His strength surprised me, and I knew I had to subdue him quickly. I grasped my gun, raised it in the air, and brought the handle down hard on his head. His head snapped to the side; a red welt began to swell where I'd struck him. He blinked his pale eyes rapidly as he fought to keep himself conscious. I rose to my feet, keeping my pistol aimed at his head.

"I'll tell you who we are: we're the ones who stop you from destroying the world," I said, breathing hard. "Now, call your men off, or I'll shoot."

"You can't stop this. If it's not me, it'll be someone else. No future can thrive with your system. It'll only end in ruin," he choked out. "Amelia will live again."

I took a moment to assess my surroundings. Tolli and Irving had recouped their weapons and were taking on five guards at once. Vee stood several feet away from me, just about to neutralize a female guard twice her size. She executed a graceful roundhouse kick to the guard's stomach and an uppercut to her chin in one fluid motion. The four agents who had come in through the roof were preoccupied with a group of guards who must have heard the blast and had rushed in to see what was going on.

In the centre of the room, amid the mayhem, Becker had disabled Amelia's shield and initiated her activation sequence.

"Vee!" I yelled.

Vee glanced over her shoulder at me, and then at Becker. She immediately understood. Blowing a wisp of hair out of her face, she ducked out of a guard's reach, flipped around, and kicked the gun out of his hand. Vee picked it up and hurled it at Becker in one smooth motion.

The gun collided with the back of his head, and he collapsed face down. Satisfied, she hurried over to help Jessie, using her momentum to slam into a guard about to shoot her friend.

Just as things were turning our way, and Cyril's men were slumping to the ground around me, something cold and hard pressed against the back of my skull.

A deep, gruff voice came from behind me, "Drop your weapon."

The voice seemed eerily familiar. I turned around and saw the face of a man I had thought I would never see again.

"Who am I?"

"You are Baba." I pointed to my father, nearly spilling my small clay bowl of mushy beans mixed with a bit of stale rice.

"That's right," he smiled, showing crooked teeth. Wavy black hair framed his bearded face. "You're very smart, my boy. Soon you'll be talking non-stop. Eat your food, so you'll grow up to be a strong young man one day."

His dark eyes examined my skinny arms and legs; we hadn't eaten in a while. Baba, Mama, and I sat on the ground in our drafty home built from scrap metal, mud, and straw. Mama shifted on the empty burlap sack she was sitting on, and her pale pink scarf started to slide off her long dark hair. Her eyebrows pinched together as she glanced at Baba.

"We need to talk," she sighed after spoon-feeding me a bite of rice. "We can't stay here."

"There's nowhere else we can go, Jola," Baba answered firmly. He stirred his rice and rested his chin on his fist, a distant look in his eyes.

"How long are we going to do this? It's been three years. What if they find—"

"You are Mama," I interrupted, oblivious to the serious expressions on my parents' faces.

"Very good." Baba patted me on the back with his rough, calloused hand. "And who are you, my boy?"

"Alex."

"Yes." He added, "You are Alex *Khanna*."

"Khaaa-na?"

"Yes," he whispered and lifted my chin. The corner of his mouth turned up in a smile as he studied my face. "That is our family name."

Pride swelled in me, and I puffed out my chest and grinned, "I am Alex Khanna."

The sight of his face flooded my mind instantly with intimate, forgotten memories. Although I had suffered from severe memory loss after I woke up at DAIR, I could never forget my father's voice. It was something a boy who had adored his father could never forget. His wiry hair was now gray, and his face was weathered with age, yet he still looked physically strong, like I remembered him. The same scruffy beard hung from his chin, and the same crooked teeth peeked out from behind his thin lips. My breath caught in my throat, and I choked down a strangled cry as the colour drained from my face.

"Baba?" I managed hoarsely.

His bushy eyebrows raised in bewilderment, and for a moment, the hardness in his dark eyes gave way to shocked recognition.

Before I could react, Cyril, still on the ground, slammed the heel of his dress boot into my gut. I doubled over in pain and stumbled backward, breaking eye contact with the father I had thought was dead for years. I looked over to see Cyril scrambling toward Amelia.

"No!" I yelled, reaching out, even though I was too far away to stop him.

I could only take a few steps before Cyril pulled down the lever on the control box. A burst of light shot from the centre of the metal disc and up into the sky through the opening in the roof.

Amelia screamed.

⇛ TERMINUS TERRA COMPLETE

Light sears through my eyes.

I try to shield myself, but all is futile.

My entire body pulses with excruciating pain.

Then, I only see darkness.

Endless, suffocating darkness intensified by failure and death.

I'm alone.

Wren is not by my side.

I am falling.

Falling.

Falling.

In the abyss between time and space, I hear a whisper that seems so familiar.

"Donna…"

But, the voice is soon forgotten as I plunge farther into darkness.

Falling faster and faster.

We thought we could change what was yet to be written.

We thought we could alter what was yet to be told.

But time has woven such an intricate web.

And we cannot escape it.

I am in awe of its complexity.

As, once again, I stumble forward and crash to my knees.

PART THREE
TREVOR TOLLI

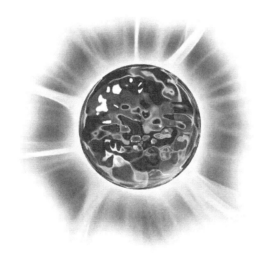

9 HOURS and 47 MINUTES to TERMINUS TERRA

October 1, 2059, 3:43 pm...

"Tolli?" Someone was calling my name.

I came to my senses with a jolt. "Yep. I'm here."

I couldn't remember what I had been thinking about. I looked over at one of our newest recruits.

"You just zoned out for a minute," Irving said and smiled, a few dark gaps visible between his teeth. "Keep it up, and we'll both be dead."

"I thought the whole point of this was to calm our nerves, not stress us out more," I grumbled and readjusted my grip on my ghost blaster.

Irving nudged my shoulder and motioned with the wide barrel of his matching weapon, complete with a green-tinted glow-in-the-dark design. He indicated with his chin that we should keep moving. We were running around in a one-block radius we'd marked off in one of DAWN's training facilities designed to look like a small, deserted town in the dead of night. Irving had my back, sweeping his weapon side-to-side as we avoided the dim streetlights. We were playing a friendly game of elimination before the op tonight. Our other two teammates had already been shot, so it was up to us to ensure victory.

Usually, Donahue wouldn't miss these types of games, but Agent Mallick had needed him to do something. Now that I thought about it, it had been quite a while since I'd last seen him.

As I was thinking of Donahue, a flash of red from beside the house across the street caught the corner of my eye.

"Irving, did you see that?" I breathed out.

"See what?"

Squinting at the house, I explained, "I saw something red over by that house with the yellow door."

"I thought the rest of our team was eliminated."

Silently, with our weapons raised and ready, we drew closer to the house, staying alert and watching each other's backs. As we neared the entrance, Agent Bree O'Connor, distinguishable by her fiery curls, peeked out from her hiding spot behind the house. A blue band was tied around her bicep and another across her forehead. Irving and I fired our ghost blasters, exchanged satisfied grins, and moved forward.

Before I knew what had happened, O'Connor suddenly appeared beside us, low to the ground. She emptied her cartridges without mercy, and Irving and I were down in an instant. A smug smile grew on her lips as the low current electrical shock discharged from the receptor in my training gear into my body. Simultaneously, our ghost blasters powered off, the glowing green components turning dark.

"Ow!" we cried in unison.

O'Connor leapt to her feet with glee and laughed, "Just be glad the paralysis agent is reserved for initiates."

"Shut up, O'Connor," Irving whined as he picked himself up.

Apparently, he hated losing even worse than I did. O'Connor blasted him in the chest a second time. A jolt of electricity passed through his large frame, causing him to sink to his knees. He gritted his teeth and glared at her.

"Blue team prevails again," she smirked, shaking her head in disapproval. "Your heads aren't in the game today, boys."

"This is a *friendly* competition and a stress-*relief* exercise," I reminded the two of them as I tossed my ghost blaster aside and offered a hand to help up Irving.

He scratched the back of his head and asked, "Well, are ya up for round...nine? It's...one–seven for the red team."

"Nah, you go ahead," I insisted while pulling back the messy strands of hair that had fallen in front of my face. "I'm gonna see if I can find where Donahue went."

Irving nodded, picked up my discarded weapon, and slung it over his shoulder. "If you do, tell him the red team could really use him."

He and O'Connor walked off, discussing different equipment in the weapons vault they wanted to try out. I ripped off my red armband and headed down the middle of the fake street, a few flickering street-lights marking the way toward the exit.

Irving had just been cleared to go on his first mission, and Mallick had mentioned he would be riding with Donahue and me in the Spar-row. I figured I should tell Donahue about our extra passenger as soon as possible. I trusted my friend knew what he was doing, but I still needed to talk to him, to work out the details.

I struggled to change out of my training gear as fast as I could and stuffed everything into my duffle bag. I had sent multiple messages to Donahue, even though I knew he didn't usually reply. He rarely carried his TetraScreen with him, and if he did, he would often "misplace" it I smiled, and then chuckled to myself as I imagined him hiding it under his mattress, and then claiming he must have "lost" it.

I scrolled through my recent messages and glanced at the time. "What the…" I muttered.

It glitched and displayed random numbers and letters. After a mo-ment, it simply read, "ERROR," so I made a mental note to drop it off at the tech lab later.

I left the training area, not knowing where to begin looking for Donahue; the complex was enormous. Fortunately, it didn't take long because he found me.

"Tolli!"

I looked over to see Donahue barrelling down the hall. He almost collided with a poor lady with big hair, scaring her enough that she dropped her briefcase. After a quick apology, he ran up to me and slid to a stop, his boots screeching against the floor.

"Tsk, tsk, tsk." I tried to give him a disapproving look, then noticed the strange uniform he wore. "Wait, what are you wearing?"

He didn't respond, not even with an eye roll. He rested his hands on his knees and, out of breath, he started, "Tolli, we—just come with me. It's urgent! I'll explain everything, but you have to come with me."

"Who's 'we'? What's the matter?" I demanded. "What's wrong?"

"A lot of things," Donahue muttered, and I detected the underlying anger in his tone.

He swivelled on his heels to sprint back the way he came, checking to make sure I was following him. He didn't need to worry; I was right behind him.

October 1, 2059, 4:22 pm...

Donahue slammed the door shut after I entered. I could tell he was extremely upset, but I had no idea why.

The tension was almost palpable in Room T-117. Mallick was seated in a plastic chair, rubbing his temples as the stress emanated from his anxious face. A russet-haired girl standing beside him was a sight to behold. She had robotics similar to Donahue's that replaced parts of her hands, neck, and cheek. She had a torn bandage taped above her eye and green eyes that looked troubled. She began pacing furiously in front of a safe behind a large, peculiar-looking metal pyramid.

Because no one was saying anything, I attempted to lighten the mood by joking to Donahue, "No idea you had a girlfriend, buddy."

"Stop saying that!" Donahue and the redhead snapped in unison.

I raised my hands defensively, surprised and confused at their outburst. I slipped into a seat and tried to make myself invisible.

"We have to talk about this first." Donahue turned to Mallick with fire in his vibrant-blue eyes. "Did you know my father was alive and working for Cyril? Did you think it was better for me to believe he was dead?"

"Donahue, I didn't—"

Donahue cut him off abruptly and shouted, "You knew I had a hard time remembering things from before the accident. You knew I couldn't even remember my name. You could have told me so many things, and you chose not to!"

When Mallick didn't respond, Donahue diverted his rage and frustration toward the wall, slamming it with both his palms. I had never seen him in this state, and I bit down on my lip. I nervously bounced my leg while the redhead twisted her hair, her gaze darting between Donahue and Mallick.

"Did you stand by while they dragged him away from me and my mom? Were you there? Is that why you and William were in my village? Did you lead Cyril's men to him?"

Donahue had only told me a bit about his past, but I did know his whole family had died before he was brought to the DAIR compound. From Donahue's aggressive questioning, I guessed his father was somehow very much alive, and he was convinced Mallick was involved.

Mallick smoothed back his cropped hair. "We weren't sure Cyril…I—no, we thought your father was dead too, but how could you know he's alive if no one else in this entire organization knows?"

"I saw him with my own eyes, and he recognized me. I…I had no idea, and I froze. That moment cost us the mission and, ultimately, the planet. They all died, Rob. Because of me! I didn't stop Amelia…"

"What are you talking about?" Mallick loudly interjected.

The redhead broke her silence and insisted, "Alex, it's not your fault."

Donahue folded his hands on his head and studied the ceiling. He spoke very slowly through a clenched jaw as if each word required a large amount of energy to articulate clearly. "Yes, it is, and you know it."

I couldn't stay quiet anymore and waved my arm to get their attention. "Hello? Can someone please tell me what's going on here?" I turned to the girl. "Red? Can you help me out? You seem like the least emotional person in here."

"My name is Wren." She opened her mouth to say more, but Donahue held up his hand to stop her.

Still glaring at Mallick, he struggled to keep his voice calm, "I'll tell you what's going on, Tolli. My father is alive and works for Cyril Elton-Blackwood right now. And I only found out about this today, at the very worst time. Rob, you have to tell me what really happened all those years ago."

Mallick's round glasses began sliding toward the tip of his brown nose as his gaze fixed on the floor. I could tell he was weighing his words carefully as he looked up at Donahue, "I'll tell you everything I know, then you need to tell me what's going on with you two."

Donahue's voice caught in his throat as he tried to suppress his emotions. He looked away, letting his hair fall into his face. Finally, he spoke, "Please, I need to know."

Mallick took a deep breath. "First off, I have to say that we didn't know he was your father. We suspected it, but when we tried to get more info from you, you couldn't remember. Will you keep that in mind as I explain things from my perspective?"

Donahue managed a slight nod, and Mallick began, "Eight years ago, we intercepted some intel leading us to believe that Cyril was looking for your father. Cyril had just left DAIR after losing his daughter, but he wasn't willing to walk away from everything he had discovered in DTS. I didn't think Cyril would have gone to such lengths to acquire an asset, but your father was no ordinary man. It's true that he was originally from the area we found you in, but he was able to get out of the cycle of poverty he was born into with his intellect, ingenuity, and persistence. Eventually, he was noticed by certain higher-ups in the military, who recognized his potential and saw the chance to benefit from his brilliance. He received the education he needed to fully develop his talents, but eventually found out about the military's intentions to exploit him. Other than William Derecho, there was no other person who excelled more in scientific innovation and discovery than your father."

Wren visibly tensed at the mention of William Derecho, but I wasn't able to put the pieces together.

"His country's military kept him a secret for years as their top man in his field, but an intellect like his couldn't stay hidden for long. When DAIR found out about all this, your father had already made a daring escape and went into hiding. You would have been very young, Donahue, so you wouldn't remember this. During his time with the military, your father realized his discoveries had made him become more of a hostage than anything else. He had grown very uncomfortable with the questionable morality of the controversial research that was being pushed on him, so he made plans to get out. I think he just wanted to raise his family free of the expectations and struggles his discoveries and abilities had caused him. But, first, he had to disappear."

Donahue looked like he was going to interrupt, but, instead, bit down on his lip and closed his eyes.

"Of course," Mallick continued, "DAIR was also interested in him, but, more importantly, they didn't want Cyril to get his hands on him. I was a field agent of DAIR back then, and they gave me the task of locating him." He paused and glanced at the redhead. "Wren's uncle, William Derecho, came with me, eager to find Xavi and talk about the work your father did before he went off the grid."

Wren winced and squeezed her eyes shut before lowering her gaze to her feet. She must have been devastated by the loss of her uncle. I felt sorry for her. William's death had been a shock to everyone; his calculations had always been precise and his research thorough. He didn't make mistakes. I had heard he'd just been in the wrong place at the wrong time. Although I didn't witness his death in person, I remembered the chaos that occurred in the week following the accident. I was only a new recruit then, but it was obvious to me that DAIR was attempting to keep the incident as quiet as possible. William was one of their biggest assets. Everyone knew that. What anyone failed to mention to me was the existence of the girl standing a few feet away, but I had begun to connect the dots. She was William's niece, she had the same robotics as Donahue, and she was somehow tied up in all this confusion.

"At the time, William was exploring the concept of an interdimensional transportation gateway apparatus, or as you know it now, Whispers of Amelia. We searched all the villages around the area we believed your father fled to. I think we made a total of five trips over a period of four years. But when we couldn't find him, we concluded that either Cyril or the military had tracked him down first. It was at this point the trail went cold as any signs of his work continuing or any intel we had about his whereabouts had grown outdated. He simply disappeared without a trace, and in this business, that usually means he'd been eliminated."

Donahue clenched his shaking fists at his sides, and I shifted uncomfortably in my chair. However, Mallick wasn't quite finished yet. "If Cyril really did take him, it's amazing he was able to keep it a secret until now, but it would also answer the question of how Cyril could pull off creating a machine like Amelia. If anyone could do it, it would be your father."

Mallick added to his initial explanation, "When we found you, we weren't certain you were Xavi's son, but we took you in, anyway. There was something about you…" He sighed, "When it came down to saving your life—"

"You made me…" Donahue trailed off, his voice seething, and gestured at Wren. "…Us into your guinea pigs for experimental robotics."

Donahue's voice cracked. He stepped back, no longer able to suppress his emotions, and stormed out of the room. Mallick stood up, knocking his chair over, but I leapt to my feet and put myself between him and the door. I held out my hand.

"No," I snapped. Donahue needed a break, and I wasn't going to have the two of them escalate things further. "Sorry, boss, but I think you should let me talk to him first."

I glanced at Wren, who had also moved toward the door, and shook my head. She pressed her lips together and looked at Mallick, who slumped his shoulders. He gave me a dismissive nod. When Wren turned back around toward Mallick, I hurried out of the room, hoping Donahue hadn't gone far.

October 1, 2059, 4:46 pm...

I wandered down the hall, replaying what had just happened in my head. Something didn't sit right about Mallick's explanation. I didn't know what had happened, but I knew whose side I was on. I clenched my fists; my heart ached for my friend.

When I was younger, my father had been my hero. It felt like we had spent my entire childhood tinkering in his garage. He had opened my eyes to the wonder of taking something old and forgotten, and transforming it into something beautiful and useful. Only later did I realize he had plans for my older brother and me to take over the family business. I wouldn't have lasted long in that lifestyle rife with shady characters and stolen vehicles. When I had chosen to work for DAWN, instead, I had to leave behind that life and the people I loved the most.

Now, thinking about Donahue, I realized the pain of losing my family had always been simmering just below the surface.

Finally, I found Donahue walking aimlessly in a small, deserted wing of the complex under construction, oblivious to his surroundings. I hung back, unsure of what to do or say. He must have sensed someone was nearby and looked up. His face was flushed as he shot a cold glance at me, and his eyes flashed a brighter shade of blue than normal.

I leaned against the wall, close enough for him to hear me, but far enough that I wasn't invading his space. "If you need a minute, that's all good. I'll wait."

Visibly shaking, Donahue curled his metal left hand into a fist, and I winced as he punched through the wall.

"Rob should have told me," he seethed, then sighed and walked over beside me.

"Feel better?"

"Not really," he grumbled, putting his back against the wall and sliding to the ground.

I joined him on the floor. "Do you need to punch another hole? Show the wall who's boss?"

He smirked, "No."

"Well, they're probably gonna tear that wall down, anyway."

He sighed again. "Tolli, I don't even know my last name."

"Wait," I cut in, "you told me your name was Donahue years ago."

Donahue avoided my gaze and stared at the floor. "Rob and I kinda made it up on the spot because I couldn't remember."

"Huh? Wait a sec, that's right! You were all flustered, and Mallick was the one who said your name was Donahue. I just figured you were an awkward sort of guy."

A faint smile tugged at Donahue's lips. "Rob has gotten me out of those kinds of situations more times than I can count."

"He's a good guy, Donahue," I reasoned. "For all his mistakes, I think he's only tried to do what's best for you."

"I know. It's just…he should have told me."

"Yeah, I bet he's regretting it now." I licked my lips, hoping I was saying the right things. It was necessary for Mallick and Donahue to get along, or things would get a lot more uncomfortable. "To my understanding, he's been the closest thing to a father to you. At least you know that part is real."

"It is."

"He's not perfect." I shrugged. "But then, no one is. And we both know that Mallick wouldn't have withheld anything from you just to hurt you. You gotta believe he was trying to look out for you."

"Yeah." Donahue took a deep breath and stood up.

I followed him up and grabbed his arm. "You don't have to go back in there if you don't want to."

Donahue nodded. "I know. But I have to. Hey, thanks...for every-thing. I'll be okay."

"You got it, buddy."

I followed him back to Wren's room. We found Mallick and Wren exactly where we'd left them. Mallick perked up and met Donahue's gaze. After a few seconds, Donahue extended his hand without saying a word. Mallick understood and shook his hand with a slight smile.

Donahue took a seat on a nearby stool. "I just needed some time...Rob, you can continue if you want."

Mallick looked apprehensive and folded his hands on his lap.

Wren picked at her lip and prompted him, "So, his name is Xavi?"

"Xavi Khanna," Mallick responded.

"Khanna," Donahue repeated, wringing his hands. He looked down. "Is my father the enemy?"

"I don't know."

Donahue pressed the heels of his palms into his eyes. "Rob, I'm not trying to accuse you of anything, but why didn't you tell me any of this before?"

"I never wanted to cause you more pain. You had a lot of tragedy and trauma in your young life at that point, and then it never felt like the right time. Besides, I was convinced he was dead, Donahue, and I wasn't even sure he was your father. You have to believe me. I'm sorry."

A long silence ensued, but I wasn't about to say anything. I may have been a talkative guy, but I had learned to keep my mouth shut in these types of emotionally charged situations. My quick wit had been responsible for getting me into trouble more times than I could count, and I was not about to add this one to the list.

Finally, Donahue lifted his head. "I know, it's just...I wanted..." He sighed, "I don't even know what I want. It's fine. I'll get over it. I just need a minute."

"Can you forgive me, Donahue?"

"Yeah."

The tension in the room dropped down a level, and Mallick's face relaxed a bit. "How in the world did you find out about him?" he inquired again and crossed his legs.

Donahue looked at Wren. "Do you want to start, Wren?"

She nodded.

This should be good, I thought to myself as I leaned forward, subconsciously hoping that leaning in would somehow clarify my total confusion up to this point.

Wren cleared her throat. "When I travelled back from changing the future, I—or something else—triggered the start of some sort of…"

"A time loop," Donahue whispered. "It's the only thing that explains why we keep reliving the same day. Okay, sorry, continue."

I stared at Donahue, shocked at how casually he and Wren mentioned travel from the future and time loops.

"Time loop?" I found myself saying my thoughts out loud. It was killing me to be quiet for so long and not ask questions. "Are you kidding me?"

I looked back at Wren, dumbfounded and unable to speak. She thought for a moment before resuming her explanation, "Yeah, I guess it is a time loop, and only Alex and I are aware of it. Every time it restarts, the timeline becomes more unstable. Anomalies in nature occurring around the world show that it's deteriorating."

The word "anomalies" triggered my memory, and I remembered how my TetraScreen kept glitching. The thought lasted only a fraction of a second as I listened to Wren's explanation.

"With every loop, the story ends in betrayal within DAWN and the failure of Operation Aquarius Deep. Cyril knows you're coming and has set a trap for your agents. During the last loop, Alex came face to face with his dad, and it gave Cyril the distraction he needed to activate his machine. Whispers of Amelia—which is also the main component of the time machine I travelled in—is triggered, and somehow, Amelia's activation and consequent explosion are linked to a massive time storm. The result is the self-combustion of the planet."

"Whoa, whoa, whoa." I held up my hand. I had found my voice, and this was getting to be too much.

I had gone along with the story about Donahue's father because I had instinctively responded to his distress. In my concern for him, I didn't have time to wonder or even ask how he came across this secret, so I had no reason to doubt its validity.

But now, with the addition of time loops and time machines, I was starting to suspect that perhaps Donahue and Mallick were trying to pull a fast one on me. It wouldn't be the first time they cooked up some sort of crazy story to lure me in only to become the butt of their joke. If they were up to something, they both deserved awards for their convincing acts. On the other hand, if the stuff about Donahue's dad was true, I would look like a total idiot—not to mention a terrible friend—if I tried to call them out on it. So, I sat there, trying to determine whether this was all true or not.

"Self-combustion? What does that mean?" I asked with an edge of suspicion.

Wren answered flatly, "Everyone dies."

"That sounds like it would make a really good sci-fi movie," I remarked, standing up and shaking my head in disbelief. "You almost had me there…good one, guys…"

I waited for them to start laughing, but they just stared at me blankly. I stopped smiling as I realized that perhaps I had misread the situation.

"Wait, you guys are being serious?"

"We knew you were going to joke about Wren being my girlfriend and that you were going to look for me after training today," Donahue replied, pushing up his sleeve.

Wren held up her wrist beside Donahue's, showing a silver-and-white watch nearly identical to his. Except hers was discoloured and cracked.

"My watch is from the future," she said, "and his is from the present. They have the same inscription: *'Aut viam inveniam aut faciam.'* In English, it means, 'I will either find a way or make one.' My Uncle William gave it to Alex a long time ago."

"Okay, no more playing. I don't want to be part of your little prank." I was getting annoyed. "I'm only going to ask you one more time. Are you guys for real?"

"Yes!" Wren and Donahue both exclaimed together.

It was still difficult to believe what they were saying, but I knew at this point they were running out of patience with my tedious questions.

"All right, all right." Mallick held up his hands between Donahue and me. "I trust you two enough to believe you're not making this up. But first thing's first. What do you know about this betrayal in DAWN?"

"That's your first question?" I blurted. "What about time loops? Time machines? Time travel?"

Mallick shot me a glance that made me shut my mouth. He asked again, "Who is the double agent?"

Again, Wren and Donahue spoke in unison, "Kyler Quan."

Donahue bit down on his lip and muttered, "I can't believe I was looking for the traitor all this time, and he ended up being the one giving me orders."

What a rat, I thought, my shock quickly shifting into anger.

Mallick groaned and slumped back in his chair in defeat, "Not Quan. We've invested so much time and effort in him. He has the potential to be an exceptional leader."

Donahue and I exchanged looks as Mallick continued, "DAWN trusted him enough to send him into the heart of the enemy territory. That decision was supported by dozens of our higher-ups, and now you're telling me he's a double agent?"

"He watched our team suffer at the hands of Cyril with a grin on his face," Donahue replied with disgust.

"I'm not surprised," I offered. "The guy's a total jerk." I'd always had a bad feeling about him, but I could never put my finger on it. "Also, I have a *lot* of questions."

The three of them looked at me like they had forgotten I was there.

My voice escalated, "You just told me you time travelled, then a bunch of science-y bad stuff happened that destroyed the world, and then you got yourselves stuck in a time loop! So now, please enlighten me: What're you gonna do about it?!"

Donahue's gaze darted over to the odd metal pyramid, then to the safe behind Wren.

"No, no…no!" She moved away from the safe. "No orb and no time machine."

I gestured excitedly at the pyramid. "Whoa! That's a real-life time machine?"

Mallick, Donahue, and Wren simultaneously answered in a tired tone, "Yes, Tolli."

Wren jumped in, "But it doesn't work. And I refuse to make it work."

A dull ache started to grow in my forehead, and I imagined my brain exploding into a million pieces. It was too much information to process.

How long had this type of technology existed? How did everyone know about it except me?

I knew I needed a break from this conversation. However, one thing stuck out from Wren's explanation that I had to ask about. "What are the anomalies you were talking about?"

Wren and Donahue exchanged quick, worried glances before exiting the room in a hurry. Mallick leapt up again from his seat, causing it to fall backward with a clatter.

As he followed them out the door, he called out, "Come on, Tolli!"

≋ 7 HOURS and 38 MINUTES to TERMINUS TERRA

October 1, 2059, 5:52 pm...

I trailed behind them, still fighting the haze of confusion and disbelief. Donahue and Wren led us to a division within the DAIR sector of the complex, the Division of Time Studies. Apparently, the study of time had begun long before I was recruited to DAWN and was still ongoing. I realized how very little I knew of the powerful organization that employed me, and I wondered how many secrets I would never learn.

I overheard Wren and Donahue speaking quietly to each other ahead of Mallick and me, thinking we couldn't hear them.

She whispered, "Are you feeling anything different?"

"What do you mean?" Donahue's voice sounded annoyed and defensive.

"You know exactly what I'm talking about: the orb."

"You don't even know if the orb has anything to do with my eyes," he insisted. "It's not influencing or controlling me. Stop asking me about that."

I found their exchange strange, but I was still processing what was happening and where we were going, so it was soon forgotten. DTS was confined to a sole corridor lined with a few rooms. The main workspace was illuminated by the numerous bright computer screens lining the walls. A small number of scientists scurried around the room, monitoring the equipment while others worked on varying sizes of TetraScreens.

Mallick signalled to a bald man with a rosy, pear-shaped birthmark on his forehead. The scientist hurried over, his oversized lab coat billowing behind him, careful not to spill his coffee.

As the man took a sip from his mug, Mallick asked him, "Giles, have the anomaly readings increased in activity?"

He nodded. "Yeah, they've increased in frequency by 10.2 percent in the last day and have climbed significantly in threat level. I was just about to file a report."

I glanced over at Wren as she steadied herself on a desk. Apparently, this news had unsettled her, and I couldn't help but notice she looked sick to her stomach.

I saw my chance to get some answers, so I interjected aggressively, "But what are these anomalies?"

Mallick adjusted his ever-slipping glasses before clarifying, "We describe them as strange, unexplainable events happening around the world that relate to the steady flow of time. This division monitors them in case DAIR needs to step in."

Giles added, "They've been occurring now for about…eight years? I'm not sure when they started, but this is the only heavy spike we've observed since the beginning. Until today, the readings were quite low, so this is very concerning."

Donahue sighed, "That's what we learned yesterday. After every reset, the anomalies seem to become more frequent and harmful to the timeline. It's possible that as it loses stability, something like a fracture in time becomes a catalyst for the growth of anomalies."

The bald scientist's brow furrowed. "Fracture in time?"

"Uh…a disruption in the timeline of sorts." Donahue began rambling, half thinking out loud to himself. "These disruptions are like… glimpses of possible routes the timeline can follow. All of them fade except for the true timeline. But if there's instability…more realities… more glimpses…these are all theories, by the way. There's still so much to learn."

Everyone else stayed silent, deep in thought, and no one wanted to mention the time loop again. Giles, not knowing what else to do, gulped down the rest of his coffee. I caught a whiff of the stale brew and wrinkled my nose at its unsavoury smell.

"So, does anyone want to tell me what the anomalies are *specifically*?" I rephrased my question, hoping someone would finally answer me.

Giles set down his cup and scratched the back of his neck. "Well, the most prevalent anomalies are dormant volcanoes becoming active without any warning, sudden shifts in climate abnormal to the region—"

"We know that already," Donahue interrupted and gripped the back of an office chair. He spoke as if reciting from memory, "The world time clock is malfunctioning, and slight tremors are shaking the planet. And there are three mysterious bursts of energy located in the threads of time which indicate its instability."

"Uh...not three," Giles corrected.

Wren's face went ashen. "H-how many a-are there now?"

"Eleven."

The faint hum of machinery around us grew in the silence that followed. Even I, who barely had any real understanding of the unsettling events of the day, knew that "eleven" sounded bad.

Donahue licked his lips and released the chair from his grasp. "Is there anything else we should know?"

Nervously, Giles adjusted his shirt collar. "Um, well, the tremors are classified as Level Two, which means the ones on the ocean floor are displacing enough water to create potential tsunamis. There isn't enough conclusive data to know how destructive they will become by the time the waves reach the coasts. The really frustrating part is that our interconnected computer networks are malfunctioning. The system is designed to sustain itself even when one of the layers crashes. The layers were put in place to prevent this kind of problem. However, for some reason, it can't recover as programmed. Power grids, communication channels, and anything connected with these networks are being affected. Simply put, failure in one area triggers the failure in another."

As if to prove his point, the splatter of dots on the digital map beside us multiplied rapidly, glitched, and finally dissipated to the original number. A couple of more dots popped up, causing some scientists in the room to respond in alarm.

Mallick pursed his lips. "Thank you, Giles. That will be all. Keep me updated if things start to spiral further."

Giles bowed awkwardly, and then turned to pick up a large file and scuttled off. Mallick motioned to the rest of us to follow him out of the room and down the corridor. He stopped just outside of DTS, away from prying ears.

"We have to stop this." Mallick crossed his arms and drummed his long, brown fingers on his bicep. "As Donahue said, things will only get worse until we fix the time loop Wren and Donahue are stuck in. This ends tonight." We all nodded in agreement. "Since we have this rare gift of foresight, we can ensure Operation Aquarius Deep will be successful. Wren, Donahue, you'll have to tell us everything you know."

Donahue nodded again and remarked, "You said the op would be successful in the past two loops, and the results were, uh, less than successful. We have to be even more thorough when we devise a strategy that uses our advantage to its full potential. Our first objective is to neutralize Kyler Quan. It'll throw them off, and we can have the upper hand immediately. Second, we need to find out where Cyril's control centre is to prevent him from hacking into our comms. We can fill in the details for the rest of the plan as we start getting ready."

He paused, so I took the chance to agree. "I think I know what you're trying to say. Your plan is for us to go on the mission as if everything's normal, and you're definitely *not* stuck in a time loop. Easy-peasy."

Wren argued, "Wait, I'm not staying behind again."

I raised an eyebrow and tried not to laugh.

Donahue put a hand on Wren's shoulder, so she'd look him in the eye. "Wren, we've already had this conversation. You're not going anywhere."

"I think I need to lead the team myself tonight." Mallick rubbed his chin, then looked at Wren. "And I completely agree with Donahue. There's no chance I'm letting you go on Aquarius Deep. Taking a civilian on a mission will erase any advantage we have. We cannot afford to make any mistakes."

"Rob, you don't have time to explain everything to Director Li and convince her to change the plan," Donahue reasoned, and Mallick squinted his eyes, shifting his attention to him. "Besides, we need you in the control centre overseeing everything. Also, it goes against protocol for the director of DAWN to go on a field op. If Kyler gets suspicious, he might act off-script, and then we wouldn't know his next steps. Stay with Wren. We need you here."

"No," Wren pleaded to Mallick, "I've stood by twice—three times if you count my journey to the future—and watched these two die in horrible ways!" She gestured toward Donahue and me. "And Cass too! I've watched as our future collapsed, and everyone disappeared."

"Shh, keep your voice down," Donahue whispered, putting a finger to his lips, and I looked around to see if anyone had heard her.

Immediately, she clamped her metal hand over her mouth and burst into tears. Mallick pulled her into his embrace, and she buried her face into his shoulder. We gave her a moment, and I busied myself with fixing my shoelaces to alleviate my discomfort.

When my patience had run out, I smiled sympathetically at Wren. "We'll be okay. All we have to do is go to the island, dispose of Quan, prevent Cyril's machine from turning on, and save the world from ending."

"Tolli," Mallick said through a clenched jaw and shook his head.

I shrugged, then massaged my temples, and squeezed my eyes shut with one last, desperate hope this was all a dream. "Man, I think I need some ice cream or something. I'll even make do with plain old vanilla. You know, before I die in a few hours."

"Tolli!" Mallick ordered, "Go take a walk."

2 HOURS and 58 MINUTES to TERMINUS TERRA

October 1, 2059, 10:32 pm...

It had taken us a little time, but, eventually, we persuaded Mallick that his presence on the island would severely compromise the mission by alerting Quan to the possibility of us knowing about him. Also, we suggested that the team needed the confident leadership of their director in their ears, overseeing their actions from the control centre. Our best bet was keeping the operation as close to the original as possible now that Donahue wouldn't be caught off guard if his dad showed up again.

Mallick issued the three of us special sets of bronze earpieces marked with a dark-red stripe. These sets had a direct line to his Tetra-Screen while still being able to switch and sync with the main comms, so we could connect with the rest of the team. The four of us spent a couple of hours talking about everything that had happened the last time, and what we needed to do to cover our bases.

However, one thing hadn't been resolved. Wren was still convinced she would be more helpful if she went along with us to Cyril's island.

"I'm coming this time, Alex," she tried again as Donahue and I strolled toward the weapons vault.

"No," he replied in a tired tone and pinched the bridge of his nose. "I thought you would understand by now. I've told you multiple times why you can't come with us. Stop bringing it up."

She tucked her messy hair behind one ear. "We already know Kyler Quan's the traitor. I can't help you anymore from here."

"Wren, you could die. You know how you can help me? By not dying."

"He makes a good point," I added, which only earned me a glare from her.

"Well, if we keep failing, we could be stuck in this time loop forever," Wren's voice intensified, "Or it could just end, and we would all die for good!"

Her voice was getting louder, so I instinctively glanced around to see if anyone had heard her, but the hallway was empty.

"No, Wren." Donahue shook his head. "No."

Wren's face grew red. She gritted her teeth and turned around, stomping furiously down the hall without turning back.

Donahue watched her for a while before he noticed me staring at him. He narrowed his eyes and spoke in an irritated tone, "What, Tolli?"

"Nothin'." I shrugged. "Just remind me never to ask your permission for anything."

That also earned me a glare from Donahue.

Upon arriving at the weapons vault, we immediately got to work gathering equipment for the mission, and since we were about an hour early, we had the whole place to ourselves. We loaded our laser tasers with short, cylindrical cartridges that glowed a deep red from the laser shells encased inside. We slipped them onto our tactical belts. I noticed Donahue hesitate as he retrieved an X-82 out of a sealed compartment in the wall.

"What's up?"

He mumbled, "I can still see the look on his face."

"Huh?" My brow wrinkled. Whose face?

"Kyler Quan's...I-I didn't have a choice." Donahue swallowed hard as he mindlessly played with the tiny explosive. "Tolli, I pressed—"

I didn't understand what he was talking about, but I felt very uneasy watching him fidget with a deadly bomb. I reached out to take it from his hand and reasoned, "Well, now we know who the traitor is, and we can stop him as soon as we see him. You—and Wren—are going to give us the advantage we need for Aquarius Deep to succeed."

He nodded and ran his fingers through his black hair, squeezing his eyes shut. "Do you ever wonder if we're doing the right thing?"

"Uh…" My voice trailed off. "What do you mean?"

Donahue had a distant look in his eyes. "Sometimes it just feels…I don't know. It's just…You know that tiny voice in your head? Telling you things feel…wrong." He shook his head and bit his lip. "Never mind."

"You good, man?"

He took a deep breath. "Yeah."

I gave him back the X-82, and he pressed it underneath his wrist. Donahue checked his watch and bent down to retie his boots.

He looked up. "You got the flash drive?"

I patted the hidden pocket on my chest. "Yeah, I got it from the IT guys. They showed me how to install it. Just wait until Cyril's program meets ours."

After joining DAWN, I'd discovered the IT department. At first, they didn't like me hanging around and always asking questions. But I grew on them like I did with most people. They realized that they couldn't get rid of me and eventually started teaching me a few things. Now, I was considered an honorary member and the coolest member of the group.

"There's no way he'll invade our network system…again."

"It'll be time to move out soon." Donahue clenched his jaw, his eyes staring blankly as he was lost in thought.

Ominously, the fluorescent lights above us flickered.

1 HOUR and 33 MINUTES
to TERMINUS TERRA

October 1, 2059, 11:57 pm...

I followed Donahue into the DAWN hanger. Relative to the size of the complex, the hanger seemed small, but it had room to house all the aircraft along with some experimental vehicles still in the testing phase. Recently, I'd overheard some DAIR engineers discussing a type of advanced cycle-vehicle nicknamed "The Wheel." They were excited that their research team had just been cleared to start building the prototype.

The massive shadow of the Osprey crept over the Sparrow as it turned toward the runway. As we drew closer, Irving walked out from behind the Sparrow to greet us.

"Irving." I had forgotten all about him.

The huge, dark-skinned man grinned, "Hey, Tolli!"

His gaze immediately wandered from me to Donahue.

As Irving opened his mouth to say something, Donahue cut him off abruptly, "Irving, I'm Donahue, and, yes, I am half-robot. Also, you're shorter than I thought you'd be."

Speechless, Irving let Donahue push past him to climb through the Sparrow's hatch. I shrugged at him as he scratched his head.

Before following Donahue in, I ran my fingers along the small rising sun insignia on the stealth craft's side. "Good to see you, little lady."

Midway through the flight, Mallick's voice emanated from the bronze earpiece in my ear, "Anomalies have increased to 11.9 percent in frequency. There are now thirteen energy bursts in the threads of time. As requested, we have confirmation that the control centre is on the fourth floor. That's the second one from the top."

Irving, oblivious to the dread we felt over Mallick's private message, glanced behind us and questioned, "Wait, did you guys hear something? From the back?"

Without waiting for an answer from either of us, he unbuckled his seat belt, turned, and opened the door to the cargo compartment.

"Hey!" Irving shouted in surprise. "Uh...guys? There's a girl back here."

Donahue and I exchanged stunned looks. Donahue jumped up as I looked back at Irving. Wren shuffled nervously beside him, and her green eyes lowered to the floor. She was dressed in a smoky gray-and-black combat jacket and matching pants.

"Wren, what are you doing here?" Donahue snapped. The frustration was evident in his tone.

"I wasn't going to stay back and be useless again." She crossed her arms defiantly. "We tried that last time."

Taking a deep breath and exhaling slowly, Donahue stepped around his seat. Irving sidestepped to let him pass and took his place beside me. Over the roar of the Sparrow's engine, we still heard snippets of their heated whispers.

Irving glanced over his shoulder, then turned to me. "Who's the girl, Tolli?"

"Well, her name is Wren, and it's a long and confusing story that I only know parts of," I admitted. "But it looks to me like she's comin' along with us."

A huge grin formed on my face. I couldn't stop it as I thought of Wren's defiance of Donahue's instructions. She was a handful, and Donahue's awkward discomfort made me chuckle.

"Is she Donahue's...uh, sister, or something?"

"What? No." I paused before adding, "I don't think so, anyway."

Suddenly, Donahue appeared between us and commanded, "Turn around, Tolli. We're going back."

"We don't have time," I said firmly, staying on course. I knew Donahue well enough to anticipate his response, so I didn't try to reason with him. "Wren will just have to come along with us. She can stay on the stealth craft."

Donahue clenched and unclenched his fists, then thumped the back of my headrest. Wren cautiously stepped up beside him, and he addressed her, "You will not leave the Sparrow under any circumstances. I'll make up an excuse for O'Connor, and she'll wait with you. We have to stay in constant contact…" He moaned and rubbed his forehead. "Rob is going to kill me if he finds out. If anything happens to you—"

"I understand. I won't leave the Sparrow," she agreed, I thought, a little too quickly.

"Sit down," Donahue commanded. "I'm not talking about this anymore."

Wren immediately strapped herself into the jump seat.

I couldn't suppress the smirk growing on my face, and I tried to disguise my laugh into a cough.

"What are you laughing at?" Donahue asked indignantly.

"Uh…I just think it's funny you think she's gonna listen to you. I've known her for a grand total of eight hours, and I can tell you it ain't gonna happen." He continued to glare at me. "Besides, what are friends for if they can't laugh at each other?"

Donahue turned away, but I could see he had softened a bit. However, I also knew he wouldn't let Wren see it. He remained standing between the seats in the cockpit. Irving, not wanting to irritate Donahue further, offered to give him his spot back, but he refused.

Irving kept himself busy on the comms. The rest of us stayed silent as Mallick briefed us and our fellow agents on the specific details of the mission.

Donahue, who was still distracted by Wren, only perked up when Mallick finished, "Agent Alex Donahue is the lead agent on this op until Quan takes over."

Irving was preoccupied with receiving updates from some other agents when Mallick spoke to Donahue, Wren, and I privately. "The anomalies are growing."

"By how much?" Donahue asked. "Are there more breaks in the threads of time?"

"According to Giles, the frequency has grown to 12.2 percent, and the areas affected are expanding away from the South Seas. The tremors are spreading and intensifying. Be careful; the interconnected networks around where you are might also affect the tech in the stealth craft. Director Li has assured me she's getting people to work on the anomaly problem. Our signals are secure, so our communication shouldn't be affected. There are still thirteen clusters of energy in the threads of time dimension, so no change there." Mallick added, "Also, Wren has run off somewhere. I don't know if she's hearing this. She's not answering any of my messages. Have you had contact with her?"

Donahue opened his mouth but didn't say anything, so I stepped in, "Nope, no clue where she is."

"Okay, let me know if you get through to her."

"Roger that."

Without another word, the speaker crackled, then went silent. The sound of wind outside the aircraft filled my ears.

Donahue turned to me. "Tolli!"

"What?"

"I'm dead. We're *both* dead," he groaned and glanced back at Wren. "We're all dead."

"If I told him the truth, he would make us turn around," I pointed out. "Then we really would all be dead."

Irving pretended he wasn't listening, but I could tell by the perplexed expression on his face that he was disturrbed. He must have thought we were crazy. Or he was crazy.

"Besides," I continued, "if everything does restart, he won't remember a thing!" Wanting to escape the present conversation, I said, "Here, Donahue, take the controls for a minute. I'm gonna teach our little stowaway how to defend herself."

"Tolli, you're just going to put ideas in her head," he critiqued, but took my seat as I slid behind him.

I assured him, "It's just for fun. I want to get to know her a little bit." I turned around to gesture to Wren. "Follow me, Red."

She smiled shyly and climbed into the cargo hold after me.

"All right, this is Tolli's Tactical Training 101, modified to teach you the absolute basics in defending yourself from a lunatic who triggered the apocalypse, like, twice already. First, this is a standard laser taser."

I grabbed the weapon off the wall. It felt light in my grasp, and I traced the red slash on it with my finger. I loaded it with a new cartridge and held it out to her.

Wren hesitated, then slowly took the laser taser. "I've never used a pistol before."

"Aim, pull the trigger, and if you hit your target, they'll experience a small convulsion before passing out. Same as shooting a pistol, but no one dies."

I gestured to the array of supplies laid out neatly in the metal cabinets. "Night goggles, smoke bombs, tranquilizing darts...you're fully stocked in here."

Donahue yelled at us from the cockpit, "I think Wren will be fine as long as she remains on the aircraft!"

I patted her cautiously on the shoulder. "Just don't shoot yourself...or me...only Donahue, if you must," I said with a wink and a grin, "and stay on the Sparrow. C'mon, Red. Let's go back out before Donahue has a heart attack."

Wren giggled and nodded.

I motioned for her to sit back in her seat and leaned forward on Irving's chair. Heavy turbulence suddenly hit us, causing me to crash into the back of his seat before stumbling backward. Irving jolted forward in his seat and gripped his armrests. I regained my balance and reached over to take the controls from Donahue and straightened the aircraft. I threw him a concerned glance and noticed his blank expression, highlighted by the bright blue gleam in his eyes.

"Hey, man, are you okay?"

"Huh? Yeah," he sighed, shaking his head and blinking rapidly. He glanced around as if he needed to remind himself where he was. "I thought I heard…never mind. It doesn't matter. Sorry. I need to concentrate on this operation, not get distracted by…other things."

I heard the pain in his tone. "Dude, I don't exactly understand what you're dealing with, but I know you're probably thinking about Xavi Khanna."

"Who's Xavi Khanna?" Irving asked, finally brave enough to join the conversation.

"He's my father…What do I say if I see him again?"

I shrugged. "If I saw my old man, I'd probably give him a hard punch to the gut, and then maybe a hug or a handshake. Depends on if he's behind bars or not."

Wren slipped out of her seat and stood up behind Donahue. She reached out to grab his metal hand. He tensed at her touch but eventually relaxed, returning her squeeze. Apparently, he didn't want to be upset with her anymore.

She gulped as sudden tears sprang up in her eyes, and whispered, "If I had one chance to see my dad…I'd tell him how much I loved him. Ian Derecho wasn't perfect, but I regret all the time I spent being angry at him." Her gaze fell to the floor as a faint smile pulled at the corner of her mouth. "He used to call me his little 'Stormy.'"

Irving perked up and exclaimed, "Wait, are you related to William Derecho?"

Wren nodded, smiling at his enthusiasm. Donahue looked away from them, blinking his glistening blue eyes rapidly. It was clear he didn't want to keep talking about his father.

Wren changed the subject, "Alex, could you run through the whole plan again?"

Grateful for the distraction, Donahue agreed. "Wren will remain in the stealth craft while we meet up with the rest of the agents and fill them in on the new intel. We have to neutralize Kyler right away—"

"Wait, what do you mean by 'neutralize Kyler'? Are you talking about Agent Quan?" Irving interrupted. "The guy who's running this mission on the ground?"

I clapped him on the shoulder, "Yeah, keep up, Irving. The new intel is that Quan is a double agent and working for Cyril."

Irving stared at me, dumbfounded for a moment, before shrugging and shaking his head.

Donahue continued, "Once he's out of the way, the Vets will secure the four watchtowers. Then, Tolli, Irving, Vee, Jessie, and I will scale the building. Irving, Vee, and Jessie will go all the way up and get in through the dome at the top that'll bring them directly to Amelia. Tolli and I will gain access to the building through a window as close as we can get to the fourth floor. We need to move fast to shut down the power from Cyril's control centre, so he won't be able to hack into our communications system back home. Then, we'll head up to where Amelia is located. The Vets should be able to back up Irving, Vee, and Jessie by that time. They'll help them get Amelia out through the roof and transfer her to the Sparrow piloted by O'Connor."

Wren finished, "Which will break this cursed time loop for good."

Irving's dark eyes widened. "Time loop?!"

≋ 45 MINUTES to TERMINUS TERRA

October 2, 2059, 12:45 am...

After we landed, Donahue, Irving, and I promptly exited the Sparrow, leaving Wren behind. Donahue assured her he would stay in contact and send O'Connor in as soon as the team was updated. The three of us quickly headed across the clearing to the rest of our team gathering by the Osprey.

Vee, dressed in her standard fitted black suit, ran up to us. A few agents were clustered around crates outside of the Osprey, waiting for further orders.

I grinned. "Oh, hey, Vee. How's island life goin'?"

"Not too bad."

Donahue cut in. "Vee, we need to speak with everyone before Kyler Quan gets here. But not over the comms. There's a—"

Agent Adeline Jessie appeared out of nowhere and unintentionally interrupted, "We're just waiting on Quan."

She swatted at a fly that landed on her cheek, smearing the camouflage paint that had been carefully applied to her face. Donahue opened his mouth to speak again, but Vee had turned to face Jessie.

She rolled her eyes, crossed her arms, and commented, "Quan's always ticked off if he has to wait for anyone. He was supposed to be here already."

"We don't want him here! He's a double agent!" I exclaimed. "That's what Donahue was trying to tell you."

Vee's gray eyes squinted in suspicion. "Quan? Are you sure?"

Donahue nodded. "I'm Donahue, by the way."

Jessie tucked a lock of blonde hair behind her ear and stuttered, "W-wait, what...What a-are we going to do then? We're supposed to be taking orders from Quan! Are you absolutely certain?"

"You're gonna have to trust us on this," I assured them.

Donahue pressed his lips together. "Rob...er, Mallick can back us up, but the comms are compromised right now. That's why he made me team leader until Kyler shows up." He checked his watch. "We have a few minutes until he gets here."

He gestured for us to follow and started jogging toward the Osprey. "Come on, guys. We have to tell the rest of the team."

Kyler Quan entered the clearing and strolled over to us. He adjusted the backpack on his shoulder and removed a silver earpiece from his ear.

"Agent Quan has joined the party," Vee murmured into her earpiece and straightened up as he approached us.

I cocked an eyebrow at her and remarked casually, "Ah, you mean the world's most charming man. Even his hair is trying to get as far away from him as it can."

"Quiet down!" Quan shouted, a scowl on his lips. "The whole island can hear you...pathetic amateurs."

As soon as he was close enough, Vee delivered a swift, bone-breaking kick to his rib cage. Quan collapsed to his knees, his face twisted in pain.

"What...do you think...you're doing?" he wheezed as he grabbed his side.

I could see the highly trained agent's shock already wearing off and being replaced with a growing fury. I knew I needed to act fast. I glanced over at Irving and saw that we were both on the same page. We jumped on either side of Quan and pushed his arms against the ground to restrain him. He only struggled for a moment before realizing he was no match for the two of us.

"Get off me," Quan snarled. "You'll pay for this."

"That's weird. I'm kinda thinking you're gonna pay for this," I retorted, tightening my grip.

"DAWN is weak; it won't survive," Quan yelled. "Cyril knows how this world works, and he's determined to come out on top. He is the future, and I'm going to take my chances with him. You would be wise to do the same."

Quan yelped as Irving turned him over and bent his arm behind him. "You're full of lies, Quan. No one here's going to listen to anything you say."

Quan yelled, "DAIR is crumbling. It won't be able to protect us. In fact, it'll be our downfall. Cyril told me everything. He knows things…"

"All right, that's enough," Vee interrupted and moved aside to let Donahue pass. "Cyril told you whatever you wanted to hear. He knows how to cheat and lie and kill."

Fear passed over Quan's face when he spotted the syringe in Donahue's hand. "No, you don't understand. There's no right side here—"

Before Quan could alert the whole island of our presence, Donahue injected the paralyzing agent called Serum J-VIII into his neck.

Quan's body trembled, and his words slurred together, "Mallick's… keeping secrets…"

Rage melted away from his reddened face as he succumbed to the drug and fell unconscious, his body convulsing slightly as the Serum J-VIII did its work. Jessie rushed over after retrieving a pair of electronic cuffs from the Osprey and clamped them over Quan's wrists.

"That should do it," I commented and dusted off my hands.

Irving easily lifted Quan's limp, lean frame and carried him into the Osprey. We agreed to keep him locked up in the brig until Aquarius Deep was finished. This time, he wouldn't be able to stand by and watch us fall into Cyril's hands.

"The Hawk is down," I reported to Mallick.

"Please repeat."

"Oh, sorry. The *mohawk* is down." I could hear scattered laughter throughout the dark field.

After a slight hesitation, Mallick's voice echoed in all our ears. "Roger that. Aquarius Deep is a go. Vets, prepare to secure the watchtowers."

As Irving hurried back from locking Quan up, Donahue turned to face the group. "Irving, Jessie, Vee, after you guys scale to the top of the building, Vee will make all the calls. Hold off as long as you can, until the Vets can back you up."

"Hope you know how to use a grappling hook, Irving," Jessie smiled, but her expression showed she felt a little uneasy after what we had done to Quan.

Irving grinned at her, also trying to ease the tension of losing a high-ranking agent, "What's a grappling hook?"

Donahue stepped toward the Osprey and looked over his shoulder at Jessie. "Jessie, make sure either you or Vee have the Circuit Toaster."

She raised her eyebrows, then pulled out a sleek white rectangle from her tactical belt. "How did you—"

"Guys, we don't have time. We need to move," I interrupted, saving Donahue from a lengthy explanation.

Jessie slipped the device back onto her belt, her face twisted in confusion. I jogged over to the crates where Donahue was heading and joined him in taking out the harnesses.

Mallick gave out orders over the comms. "Jessie, Irving: east side. Viola, Tolli, Donahue: west side. Head out now. The watchtowers should be secure as soon as you arrive."

The five of us approached the stone fortress, shielded by the cover of darkness. I dropped the heavy duffle bag I'd been carrying as Irving and Jessie continued to the east wall.

"Team Jerving!" I heard Jessie cheer quietly as they ran away.

"I haven't used one of these in a while," I admitted to Donahue as I studied the heavy grappling gun I had been carrying.

"Me neither, and you know how much I hate heights," Donahue responded as he clipped on his harness buckles. He gritted his teeth and whispered, "Hold on tight."

Vee came up behind us, looking confident and calm. She closed one eye, aimed her grappling gun at the top of the building, and pulled the trigger. A piece of sharp metal, shaped like a lotus flower, flew out of the wide barrel and embedded itself near the top of the stone wall. Attached to it was a polyethylene-based rope, manufactured to be thirty-four times stronger than steel. Like clockwork, Vee fastened the grappling gun to her harness.

I applauded. "Nice shot."

"Meet you guys up there," she called out as she pressed the retracting button and was promptly whisked upward.

The initial burst from the retractor took her about two stories up the wall, and in one smooth motion, Vee's feet hit stone, and she started climbing up with the help of the rope. The grappling guns were known for being difficult to manage on the run, yet Vee's transition was effortless, hinting that this girl had some remarkable skills. Donahue and I exchanged impressed glances before quickly shooting our grappling guns. I jabbed the button, and the ground fell away as I ascended into the chilly night air. The wind tore at my hair for a moment before the soles of my boots hit the wall.

Feeling the adrenaline pump through my veins, I smiled and looked over at Donahue, who tried to keep his gaze from straying to the ground. He pulled at his jacket sleeve to check his watch for the umpteenth time.

"I should probably give Wren an update," he said, breathing hard. He held the rope with one hand and adjusted his earpiece with the other. "Wren, we're scaling the building now. Everything good there?"

Donahue had altered his bronze earpiece, so only he could talk to Wren. He mumbled a few things before relaying to me, "She's okay."

I nodded and glanced up at Vee, who was a little farther up, but not quite in earshot.

"What are you going to do about your dad?" I asked Donahue.

He adjusted his grip and continued climbing beside me as our ropes aided in pulling us steadily upward. "What do you mean?"

I clarified, "If you see him again, what are you going to do?"

Donahue didn't answer me, and I didn't push him. Eventually, we caught up with Vee.

"You guys are slow," she remarked and flattened her lips into a straight line. "Jerving is almost at the top already. And who's Donahue talking to? I can't hear him on the comms."

"Uh…"

Thankfully, I didn't have to answer her.

Vee was focused on Donahue and me as we came up to the ledge, so I noticed the mortar crumbling under the sole of her boot before she did. I swiftly leaned over to grab her arm as she struggled to get a good grip on her rope, swinging past me. Her question was forgotten as she concentrated on regaining her footing.

"I'm fine, Tolli," she insisted and pulled her arm away from me in embarrassment. "I just stepped on a loose piece of rock."

"You're welcome. I guess you owe me one." I grinned and quickly shifted as she playfully reached out to punch me. "Race ya up."

Vee and I quickened our pace to catch up to Donahue.

He paused and motioned, "Vee, you go on ahead, and we'll see if we can get in through that window."

Vee nodded and continued upward while Donahue and I climbed toward the window. I retrieved a miniature laser glass cutter from the pack on my tactical belt and went to work cutting a large circle out of the glass. Donahue used a suction cup to carefully push in the glass and slipped inside. I followed suit and took off my harness. I looked around the large office space we had broken into.

Donahue adjusted his earpiece once again and spoke to Mallick and the rest of the team, "Tolli and I are inside the building."

Curious, I leaned over the cluttered "C"-shaped desk to look at an aged picture frame. It had been placed on the edge of the desk between a stack of files stamped "TOP SECRET" and a black revolver. Through the glass, split in half by one large crack, the image showed Cyril standing beside a tall, dark-skinned woman holding a young girl with colourful clips in her frizzy hair. Cyril and the child looked so happy; however, the identity of the woman remained a mystery as the corner of the photograph was folded over her face.

"Tolli, let's get moving," Donahue urged, jolting me out of my thoughts.

I tossed the picture aside, but I couldn't help but wonder how devastating it would be to lose a child.

After drawing our laser tasers, we crept out of the room, keeping our heads down and moving fast, even though there was no way to completely avoid the security cameras. My heart thumped against my rib cage as I followed Donahue down a dimly lit corridor that eventually widened and came to an area with multiple doors. Donahue counted the doors and motioned to the one with a bright, blueish-green glow coming from beneath it. A shadow passed under the metal door, and Donahue held a finger to his lips. We each took a side.

At his signal, we burst through the door, taking the three technicians inside completely by surprise. After we knocked them all out with our laser tasers, Donahue closed the door, and I took a seat in front of the multiple computer screens crowding the back wall. Before I could touch anything, the feeds glitched, blanked to a purple hue, then displayed the main room on the top floor, where Irving, Jessie, and Vee surrounded Amelia in the dark room.

I cracked my knuckles and went to work.

It only took me a few minutes to find the program designed to take down our communications. It was obvious they didn't expect company as I was able to easily access their encrypted files. I said a silent thank you to my IT pals.

I told Donahue, "Cyril has some kind of malware he launched from these computers that invades the targeted system, takes control over it, and then syncs it with his. That might explain why he had to broadcast the…execution. He needed time for his program to upload to take complete control over our comms."

"Can you stop it?"

Suddenly, Amelia's room lit up, and guards swarmed around Vee, Irving, and Jessie. Donahue tensed up beside me and inhaled sharply.

Mallick's deep voice filled our ears, "Vets, where are you? We need backup for the extraction team ASAP! Donahue, Tolli, you need to move. Get up there."

"Roger," I replied and answered Donahue's question, "I can stop it. It hasn't been launched yet, so I can disable it with this little guy."

I retrieved my flash drive from my hidden pocket.

Shouts and heavy footsteps came from outside the room. Donahue glanced over his shoulder, annoyed. "I think we've got company. I'll take care of it."

Keeping my eyes on the screens in front of me, I heard guards enter the room, and then thumps as bodies hit the ground.

Donahue grunted, "Hurry up, Tolli."

"This thing's slow." Impatient, I tapped my fingers beside the keyboard. Out of the corner of my eye, I saw Donahue smash the butt of his weapon into some poor guy's face. "Cyril should really update these computers."

I froze as a click came from behind me, and something hard jabbed into the back of my skull. "Uh, Donahue?"

"Give me one sec," he called out.

"Get up and turn around." I slowly stood with my hands raised and turned to see a brawny female guard with bright-purple hair aiming her handgun at my nose. She commanded, "Step away from the desk."

Just as I was about to step back, the guard collapsed to the floor, spasming as the laser bullet did its trick. Behind her, Donahue wiped the blood on his lip with the back of his hand and looked up at me.

Before I could ask if he was okay, Donahue tilted his head toward the computers. "Tolli."

"Oh, right." I hurried to finish what I started. "Perfect timing."

A few long seconds passed before the fluorescent lights above us powered off, and the computer screens blanked, thrusting us into darkness. The backup generators powered up, triggering a row of dim red lights to pulse outside the room.

There was just enough light for me to see Donahue racing toward the door. I immediately followed, and we sprinted out of the room, heading toward the stairs leading up to the top floor.

≋ 5 MINUTES to TERMINUS TERRA

October 2, 2059, 1:25 am...

Donahue and I burst in on the chaos in Amelia's room just as Vee sent a series of kicks to a guard's face. Irving and Jessie fought side by side, taking on a group of four guards. The Vets, sent as backup, had already shown up—obvious by the shattered glass at the top of the dome—and were fighting the crowd of guards that had come from other parts of the building.

To our left, menacing bodyguards shielded Cyril with guns raised and ready for action. They slowly moved toward the exit, keeping to the edges of the circular room. No one saw us as we ducked behind some storage shelves and stealthily made our way toward Cyril.

Donahue signalled for me to stop and pulled the X-82 off his wrist. He took a moment to survey the scene, and then tossed the bomb at some machinery close to Cyril and his men. The small disc stuck to the metal with a click, and Donahue detonated it immediately. The explosion sent guards flying, shrapnel shredding through their uniforms.

After shielding himself from the blast, Donahue rushed over to neutralize a very surprised and dazed Cyril, who had his hands clamped over his ears. Drops of blood seeped through his fingers, and I guessed his eardrum had ruptured. Donahue wrapped an arm around Cyril's neck and dug a small pistol into the back of his skull. I was closing in behind him, but out of nowhere, a tall guard with a goatee stepped in between us and raised his gun. Before he could get a shot off, I fired my laser taser, and the red shell nailed him between the eyes.

I kept my finger on the trigger as I scanned my surroundings and kept moving toward Donahue and Cyril. I spotted a black-clad figure running up behind Jessie as she was preoccupied with another guard, so I aimed my weapon across the room and took him down. DAWN was gradually overpowering Cyril's forces, and I smiled as the tension began to fade. Victory was on the horizon.

Suddenly, I heard a familiar feminine voice yelling behind me, and I glanced over to see Wren, her laser taser in hand. My gaze darted back to Donahue; he didn't notice her.

There was a hardened look in his blue eyes. One filled with hate and rage. It was a look I had never seen before on my friend's face. He emptied the rest of his rounds, and Cyril collapsed to the floor, twitching, blood splattered across his body.

I froze, unable to process the scene in front of me. Wren appeared beside me. A scream escaped from her throat, and I turned my head to see an older man with a scraggly beard walk up behind Donahue, his pistol trained on his back. The man had the same caramel-brown skin tone. All I could do was watch as Xavi Khanna fired his gun, and the bullet struck Donahue and passed through his chest.

Donahue looked down at the dark-red blotch growing on the front of his shirt and turned to face his father. He choked out, "Baba," before collapsing to the ground.

≋ TERMINUS TERRA ACTIVATED

October 2, 2059, 1:30 am...

"**B**uddy. Donahue. Look at me. Please. Please, don't die."

I knelt beside his limp body, angry tears blurring my vision. I pushed my hands firmly against his wound, but I couldn't stop the bleeding. His once vibrant-blue eyes had been reduced to a lifeless, dull hue. I heard hesitant footsteps as someone walked up next to me. I turned to see Wren. All the colour had drained from her face.

The fighting came to a halt as Cyril's guards realized their leader was dead. DAWN had won, but victory had come at a great cost. I struggled to fill my lungs with air. As I gasped with each short breath, my shock turned to rage. My heart rate shot up, and my pulse throbbed in my ears. Shaking, I curled my hands into fists as burning anger enveloped me.

"He's your son, Xavi! You killed your own son!" I yelled hoarsely at Xavi, who stood stone-still in the same place.

His finger was still on the trigger, but his hands shook. Stringy gray hair fell over his shocked face.

Xavi's deep, accented voice quivered, "No, impossible. My son is dead!" Tears welling up in his dark eyes, he fired back, "DAWN murdered him and the rest of my family! That is not my son!"

"This can't...this can't be real," Wren mumbled under her breath and squeezed her eyes shut. "I have to make things right."

Before my brain processed what she meant, a rumble came from beneath us. I looked down, and the ground began to tremble. After a few seconds, the tremors split the concrete I was standing on. I jumped to the right and steadied myself, thinking back to Giles and what he'd said about the anomalies.

I looked up to see Wren lurch forward. A deep crack in the floor widened in front of her, and she swiftly leapt over it. All around me, I could see fear and confusion written on everyone's faces. Agents and guards tried to keep their balance and avoid the shifting tiles as the ground continued to quake. Some screamed as the floor gave out beneath them, and they plummeted below.

I noticed Wren racing toward Amelia, and I shouted, "WHAT ARE YOU DOING?!"

I braced myself to follow her, but I was instantly distracted by the sound of an aircraft above the dome. The Sparrow, visible through the broken glass in the roof, sputtered and burst in a series of electrical sparks. I stared, wide-eyed, as it spun around before falling out of the sky, a trail of black smoke billowing behind it. There was one last roar of the engine before I heard it crash against the building's weakened foundations, and I saw the burst of flames leap out from behind the black clouds of smoke. The explosion shook the walls, and spiderweb cracks grew on the remaining glass of the dome. Shards of jagged glass began dropping down around us.

I winced as falling glass sliced my skin through my sleeves, as I shielded my head with my arms. I pushed past the pain and stumbled toward Wren. I suddenly realized what she was about to do and knew I had to stop her. She hesitated momentarily, then began turning dials and pushing buttons on Amelia. The controls lit up as I staggered up beside her, but I was too late.

She pulled the lever.

I shouted and braced myself, waiting for the explosion. But nothing happened. Amelia went dark as glass and concrete continued to pour down on us and the building tore itself apart.

"We're out of time," I realized.

A thunderclap sounded overhead, and a blinding flash in a wide spectrum of light engulfed us. I shielded my eyes with my hands to no avail as an invisible wave of energy sent me flying through the air.

We had been wrong about everything. We had failed before we had even begun. The apocalypse did not need to be initiated by Amelia; it was guided by the mysterious hand of fate.

But, I would have no memory of any of it.

"Tolli?" Someone was calling my name.

I came to my senses with a jolt. "Yep. I'm here."

I couldn't remember what I had been thinking about. I looked over at one of our newest recruits.

"You just zoned out for a minute," Irving smiled, a few dark gaps visible between his teeth. "Keep it up, and we'll both be dead."

PART FOUR
ROB MALLICK

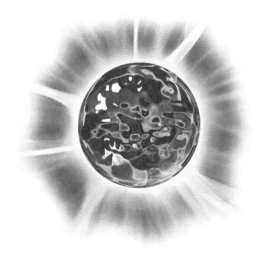

October 1, 2059, 3:43 pm...

As Donahue rose from the ground and looked at me warily, I immediately knew something was wrong. I had known him since he was about twelve, and I was the closest thing to a father he had in his life. We'd had our share of serious talks over the years, especially after William Derecho died.

"Donahue, what's wrong?" I asked, wide-eyed.

"Rob, I—" He looked down, ran a hand over his chest, and gulped down a few deep breaths.

He didn't get a chance to finish as Wren swung open her door. She choked out a sob at the sight of him, and to my surprise, they embraced tightly.

"Wren, what happened?" Donahue broke away from her. He subconsciously pressed his palm against his heart again.

"It's okay, Alex. It restarted. We have another chance."

He sighed and gritted his teeth, groaning, "My head is pounding. Everything is starting to run together, like we're getting bombarded with glimpses of alternate timelines before they fade away."

"Wait, you two know each other?" I cut in.

I had been looking after these two for years, and I had made a conscious decision not to tell either of them about the other yet. It had never felt like the right time, and I was concerned about how Wren would react. The two of them had experienced so much tragedy in their young lives, but Wren had been having a much harder time than Donahue. Sometimes she wouldn't talk to me for days. I couldn't risk introducing someone into her world who might trigger resurfacing anger she already struggled to control.

However, those fears were soon forgotten as I watched how comfortable they were with each other. Even so, my confusion remained. "What's going on, guys?"

Donahue turned to me. "We'll explain everything, Rob, but first, I need Wren to tell me what happened in the last loop. I don't remember the end of it. Wren, why didn't you guys stop Amelia?"

"Loop. Amelia." I repeated to myself, my mind whirling as I tried to piece together what was happening.

"It wasn't Amelia like we thought…" Wren's voice drifted off, and she avoided Donahue's gaze. "This time, it wouldn't activate, even though it was turned on."

"Wait, how do you…" Donahue's voice escalated, "You tried to reset everything?!"

"It doesn't matter now."

"Wren, that could have been our last chance!"

"It doesn't matter because it didn't work. Amelia didn't trigger the time loop," she retorted, the level of her voice rising to match his. "And why did you shoot Cyril, Alex? That wasn't the plan! You…you *killed* him!"

"You killed Cyril?" I exclaimed in utter disbelief.

Donahue's explanation only made me more confused. "Yes…no, he's alive now." He turned back to Wren. "You could have killed all of us for good."

Tears glistened in Wren's eyes, and she quickly wiped them away. "Well, I didn't. And your dad might not have shot you if you hadn't decided to kill Cyril. So, we both did things we shouldn't have done!"

"You're unbelievable! You shouldn't have even been there!" Donahue yelled.

"Stop arguing! Obviously, something big is going on here, but I can't help the both of you if you don't calm down." My temple throbbed as I felt my blood pressure rise. Raising a family had not been a part of my life plans, but between these two kids, I felt like I had my hands full.

Wren gulped. "Alex, I think we have to escape your way by using Tempus II and the orb."

"Did you just say…" My voice trailed off as Wren and Donahue looked in her room. I followed their gaze to the metal pyramid of the time machine.

I decided it was time to take control of the situation and adjusted my glasses. "Okay, that's it. I need an explanation from you two this instant! Get inside the room and sit down. Then, you will answer all these questions for me, in this order. What is going on? Who died? And what in the world does Whispers of Amelia have to do with any of this?"

Donahue and Wren exchanged glances before they both turned and entered Wren's room. I followed them inside, expecting answers, only to find that I had even more questions.

"Wren, what happened to your room?" I gestured to the toppled tables and papers scattered across the space. As I turned to meet her gaze, my eyes widened as I noticed her face was injured. "What happened to your face?"

She carefully brushed a finger over the scab above her eye before she answered, "Oh, it's not new. I must have lost the bandage. Anyway, Dr. Flores already looked at it."

I threw my hands up in frustration as Donahue spoke up. "We don't have much time, Rob, so here's the gist of it. It all started when Wren travelled to the future. She had no choice but to alter the timeline because of where it was headed. When she returned, she found herself in this new timeline mysteriously distorted by a time loop. For some reason, only Wren and I are aware of these loops. Interestingly, the start of each loop coincides with the launch day of Operation Aquarius Deep. Part of the reason the op fails each time is because of Kyler Quan's treachery. But, even when we stopped him, something else went wrong."

Donahue paused to catch his breath. "We've also discovered that my father is alive and works for Cyril; in fact, he's likely the one who built Whispers of Amelia. Each time, we thought Amelia created and bonded with a time storm that caused the planet to self-combust and also somehow triggered the time loop. But, according to Wren, that's not the case. We now know it doesn't matter if Aquarius Deep succeeds or fails as we're still stuck in the same day following Wren's initial arrival from the future. So, since stopping Amelia doesn't help, the only other plan we can think of is what we had decided would be our last resort. We have to finish Wren's time machine and try to push the timeline forward."

"I just...I don't..." I sighed, removed my glasses, and pinched the bridge of my nose. My knees felt weak, so I walked over to a plastic chair and sank into it. I thought for a while. "All right, I trust you two enough to believe you're not making this up. But this...this is a lot to take in. Quan's a double agent? We've invested so much time and effort into him. I just need a little time to process all this information."

I had known Kyler Quan for four years since he was first recruited. My colleague, Agent Silvia Mercier, and I had hand-picked him during his final assessment because we saw so much potential in him. Aside from some complaints regarding his interpersonal skills, Quan was an exceptional, high-ranking agent who had always been devoted to DAWN.

If the thought of Quan betraying us wasn't enough, news of Donahue's father being alive had me at a loss for words. I had never met the man, but I had certainly heard about his extraordinary groundbreaking work in the study of time, relayed to me extensively by William Derecho when he was alive. I was the agent charged with locating Xavi Khanna, but I'd never been able to find him in the five years preceding Donahue's accident. The man sure knew how to go off-grid, and if he was still alive today, he had remained hidden for over eight years. We had met Donahue a few years after Xavi disappeared; he was just a scrawny kid trying to survive without his parents. William had been the one to recognize the similar features Donahue shared with Xavi. Their characteristics and mannerisms were remarkably consistent, and we both agreed it was highly probable that the boy belonged to Xavi. However, we weren't completely certain without DNA testing.

By chance—or, perhaps, fate—we found Donahue again a year later on the day he got seriously injured from a near-fatal fall. Following his accident, William had been filled with compassion for the poor kid and had taken him in because he knew it was the right thing to do. That was the type of man William was.

I grimaced as a sharp pain stabbed my chest. I still felt the grief of losing William two years after the explosion of Tempus, the first time machine prototype, that had taken his life. He had been my closest friend, and a day hadn't gone by since his passing that I didn't miss him.

Donahue, also deep in thought, rubbed his temples, then suddenly recalled, "Kyler said something about there being no right side. He told us that DAIR wouldn't be able to protect us and Cyril told him every-thing…Do you have any idea what he was talking about, Rob?"

"How did he…" I frowned, then shook my head. "I don't. I have no idea what Cyril would have told him. I suspect Cyril would have told Quan anything if he thought it would benefit himself. As long as I've known Quan, he's been loyal to DAWN."

"Well, Cyril turned him somehow," Donahue pointed out.

Wren chimed in, "Could it have been about something DAIR was doing that he didn't agree with?"

"I'm not sure what were lies and what was sincere. It's hard to tell with Kyler." Donahue turned from her to face me again. "Are you ab-solutely certain you don't know what he was referring to?"

"I already said I don't know."

"Really?" His eyebrows raised. "His last words before the drugs kicked in were 'Mallick's keeping secrets.'"

I stared at him, speechless. Taken aback, I wondered if Quan had alluded to the secrets about the orb. DAIR was full of confidential mat-ter, and I knew there were things I needed to tell them, but now was not the right time. It would have to wait until after this crisis was over.

Wren picked at her lower lip, then began, "Do you think he knows about my uncle and the orb—"

She suddenly rushed to the back of her room to open the small safe on the ground. She retrieved the blue orb her uncle had been so invested in and headed back to Donahue and me. Donahue stared at the small, mesmerizing object, and he clenched his fists at his sides.

"Wren," I said, remembering why I wanted to speak to her in the first place, "that thing is hurting you. You know how to handle the orb better than any of us. But, like we talked about earlier—"

"Rob, you don't have to worry about me," Wren assured me and tucked the orb into her pocket. "As soon as we break the time loop, we'll figure out how to get rid of it forever."

"We don't need to rush into anything, though. We might need it later on," Donahue quickly suggested. "Anyway, for now, we need to focus on today. On getting out of this loop. I don't know how many more chances we'll have."

Their calmness in this situation perplexed and concerned me. I wondered how many times they had lived this day. I hesitated. "What do you mean?"

"Oh, yeah, the anomalies," Wren replied, stepping closer to me. "Rob, we need to check on those at DTS. With each loop, the timeline becomes more and more unstable. If we don't succeed in breaking out of it, it's possible the whole timeline will collapse at some point."

Donahue clarified, "That was a possibility in all the loops, but this is now the third one, which means we'll have to act faster. I think using the time machine is our only option."

At this point, I was faced with two choices: believe them completely or walk away.

"So, what do you propose we do?" I questioned, rubbing my temple with one hand. "How can I help?"

"First, we need to find Tolli—he's looking for me right now—and fill him in on everything. Then we need to figure out a new plan to steal Amelia as soon as possible, so we can bring her back here to finish building Tempus."

Before Donahue could run off, I reached up and grabbed his arm, "Donahue, your dad…I never told you. I didn't know he was still alive."

"You told me everything in the last loop."

"He would have been so proud of you, Donahue," I said and released my grip. "I didn't know much about him, but I did know he loved his family. A lot. I'm sorry I didn't—"

"It's okay, Rob. I know you did what you could," Donahue smiled and nodded to reassure me. He swivelled on his heels. "I'm going to get Tolli. I'll be right back."

Tolli shook his head and chuckled. "That sounds like it would make a really good sci-fi movie. You almost had me there…good one, guys…"

Donahue had found Tolli and caught him up on everything he and Wren had told me. As expected, Tolli was skeptical—with good reason. Oddly, only Wren and Donahue were aware of the time loop. They carried the heavy burden of having to repeatedly convince everyone of the impending crisis, including me.

When we stayed silent, Tolli's childlike grin disappeared. "Wait, you guys are being serious?"

"It's very confusing," I admitted, "but I think Donahue and Wren are telling the truth. We don't have time to joke around. We need to help them break the time loop."

Donahue added, "Rob's right. We don't want to argue, Tolli. It took you a while to believe us in the last loop, but we don't have time to go through it all again. I wouldn't lie to you about this."

Tolli took a moment to process everything and narrowed his eyes in suspicion. "This isn't funny, guys. No more playing. I don't want to be part of your little prank. Seriously, your dad, Donahue?"

"This is real," Donahue persisted. "The clock is counting down until the world ends, and everyone dies. If you want proof, think about it. I knew exactly where you were after training and why you were looking for me. You wanted to tell me that the recon team on the island just contacted the control centre, and Cyril doesn't suspect a thing—which is wrong, by the way. I know you wanted to tell me Dean Irving was flying with us to the island." Tolli blinked hard at Donahue's sudden serious tone and let him continue. "I know every dumb joke you're going to make, but please don't make me repeat them all. I just need you to trust that I'm telling you the truth."

He stared at Donahue before finally nodding, his mop of blonde hair bouncing. "Fine. I'm in, but if this is a joke, I'm going to punch you…like, five times…right in the teeth. Got it?"

Donahue smirked. "Deal."

I stepped in. "So, what's the plan?"

"I think we need to leave for the island immediately," Donahue responded. "We need all the time we can get."

Wren picked at her bottom lip. "Then I need to stay and work on modifying Tempus II to incorporate Amelia and the orb as a power source."

Donahue cocked an eyebrow. "Really, Wren? No arguing? No tricks this time?"

She shook her head. "I'll be way more useful here. No tricks, I promise."

"Okay." He looked satisfied.

I didn't have a clue what they were alluding to, and I wondered in what reality Wren would be allowed to go on a DAWN operation. Then it occurred to me that she was wearing different clothes from earlier…an outfit like some of my agents wore out in the field. I shook my head; there was too much I didn't know, and maybe it was better that way.

I sighed. Even if we found a way out of this mess, I was sure these kids were going to be the death of me.

Smiling, Donahue patted her on the shoulder and turned to Tolli and me to continue. "All right. Wren stays here with Rob, and we'll keep in contact. Tolli and I will just need to gather a few things before we—"

"Wait," I interrupted, holding up my hand to stop him. "I'm not leaving the fate of the world in your hands. You need help. I'm going with you."

Donahue countered, "Rob, do you think that's a good idea? We don't have time to explain everything to Director Li and convince her to revise this op at the last second. And if it comes to that, you have to be the one to do it. It also goes against DAWN protocol! We need you here to run the mission in case something happens to us."

"You think you'll be able to pull this off by yourself? The two of you? No, you need me there. The recon team trusts me completely. If

I'm there on the ground giving orders, they won't question me. You said time is of the essence."

"Mallick makes a good point, man," Tolli commented.

Donahue's gaze wandered to Wren. She agreed, "I think so too. It'll go faster with Rob giving orders there. I'll be fine here by myself."

Donahue took a deep breath before outlining his revised plan, "Okay, let me think. Tolli, Rob, and I take the Osprey and the Sparrow and meet up with the other four agents already on the island. This time, we're going for speed and stealth, so forget about Kyler. We get in through the glass dome at the top of the building, get Amelia, and get out."

"Since we have to take down all the watchtowers anyway, why don't we zip-line down from one of them to the dome?" Tolli suggested. We all looked at him, and he shrugged. "What? We did something similar in training a few months ago, remember? It would be the fastest way, right?"

"Yeah, that's actually a great idea," Donahue commended him. "Once we're in, we get Amelia out and transfer her to the Sparrow. We get out ASAP and head back here to help Wren attach Amelia to the time machine. Once that's done, I think it would make sense for Wren and me to travel forward in time to push the timeline past where it keeps looping. We have an advantage because we're not a part of the loop in the first place, meaning if something goes wrong, our memories won't be reset."

"I wonder what will happen to the rest of us during that time jump..." Tolli's voice trailed off as he chewed the inside of his cheek.

"Honestly, we have no idea," Wren admitted, then added, "We're hoping the timeline gets corrected, meaning you may not remember it, and time will continue as if everything was normal. We would only be jumping forward..." She glanced at Donahue. "Half an hour?"

"Umm, let me think about that." Donahue paused and pressed his lips together. "I'm not sure...an hour, tops."

"Huh." Tolli scratched the back of his head and joked, "Well, losing an hour of my life is not so bad. I've watched some crappy movies that made me lose double that."

Wren smiled.

"But, what about Xavi?" Tolli asked as he looked at his friend with sympathy.

"I…we—we don't have time." Donahue's voice cracked as he swallowed hard and rubbed his forehead. "Our only goal right now is to make it past zero-one-thirty hours. But first, we really need to check in with Paris Giles about the anomalies."

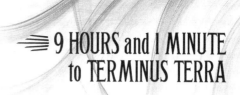

9 HOURS and 1 MINUTE
to TERMINUS TERRA

October 1, 2059, 4:29 pm...

We found DTS in a state of pandemonium. Dozens of scientists scurried in every direction, poring over files and frantically working on TetraScreens and various monitoring equipment.

"Where's the digital map?" Wren wondered out loud.

Director Li stood in the centre of the disarray with Agent Silvia Mercier by her side, consulting with two frustrated scientists. Mercier's white hair was pulled back into a tight ponytail, exposing the grave expression on her face.

"Director Li," I called out to her, "what's happening here?"

Director Li didn't look up at me as I approached her since she was preoccupied with her large TetraScreen. As she tapped the screen aggressively, she replied, "Now's not a great time, Director Mallick. I'm not sure what's happening, but it's bad, and I need to figure out what we're dealing with. I'll brief you as soon as I can regarding the security side of things."

Director Li turned her back to me, and her high heels clicked as she rushed to the other end of the room. Her normally perfect hair looked dishevelled, and the stress of the last hour or so was evident on her face.

Wren, Donahue, and Tolli quietly approached me, glancing around the chaotic room. Scientists hurried about as they shouted to one another. My head spun as I could feel the fear and tension encompassing the room.

I turned to Mercier. "Why are you here? Did Director Li ask you to assist her?"

Mercier was my second-in-command. We'd been recruited around the same time and had moved up the ranks together. I remembered flying over a drop zone on our first mission and watching her jump out of the aircraft into the foggy night without a trace of fear on her face. I had admired her from the first day we met, and a lot of assumptions were made about us because of how much time we spent together. But we were never more than good friends. In this business, our work was our top priority. Mercier was exceptionally qualified and the best senior agent I could ask for to stand by my side. However, as I stood next to her now, I could tell she didn't seem too happy to see me.

"I was looking for you." She crossed her muscular arms and looked up at me. "You haven't been answering my messages. We've lost all contact with the DAWN agents on the island, and our interconnected networks are starting to crash. Director Li has her hands full with DTS, so I didn't really want to fill her in until after I talked to you. You really should be checking your TetraScreen, Mallick."

I cleared my dry throat as she relayed the concerning news. "Mercier, I didn't get any messages. What is Communications doing to reconnect with the team?"

I patted my shirt pocket and furrowed my brow; my device was hot to the touch. During the craziness of the past hour, I hadn't noticed the heat radiating through my shirt. I pulled it out and was confronted with a blinking "ERROR" message on the glassy screen. I tried to restart it, but the device refused to comply.

Mercier looked over my shoulder and sighed, "Just take this."

She picked up a TetraScreen from a nearby desk and tossed it to me, then answered my question. "I've got them working on it. Something's affecting the electrical signals. I don't know if we'll be able to reconnect, or if the agents have been compromised. Do we need to send a team there?"

"Maybe. Let me think about it. If we do, I'll take care of that," I assured her.

Donahue was the first to join in on our conversation. "Agent Mercier, do you know where we can find Paris Giles? We need to speak with him."

Mercier directed us to the far corner, where the bald scientist was concealed behind a tower of equipment. "Mallick, keep in touch. Can we meet back in the control centre when you're done here?"

I nodded, and Mercier quickly left the room. I turned around and walked toward Giles, and the rest of the group followed me. Giles was rolling his chair back and forth between two large computers. Beside him, empty paper cups reeking of stale coffee were stacked high.

"Giles, give me an update on the anomalies."

Startled, he jumped in his seat. He glanced up at us, and then back at his screen. His hands shook as he pulled up a world map covered with red marks.

"There's no point tracking them anymore. The last time I checked, they were increasing in frequency 29.7 percent every hour. Things are getting out of control."

"How many explosions of energy are in the threads of time?" Wren questioned. "I'm guessing it's more than thirteen?"

"Our last estimate was fifty and growing."

I assumed only Tolli and I didn't understand the weight of the number; it appeared Wren and Donahue certainly did as their jaws dropped.

Tolli cut in, "So, what are these anomalies?"

"It doesn't make sense. This kind of damage from natural disasters has never happened in the eight years I've worked here. We're trying to figure out exactly how they tie into the linear flow of the timeline," Giles said as he looked warily at me.

"But what are they, exactly?" Tolli persisted.

Giles pulled at the collar of his green polo shirt, sweat collecting on the back of his neck. "The tectonic plates are shifting unnaturally and violently, causing towering tsunamis and land masses to break apart. Volcanoes are erupting simultaneously, and massive tornadoes are forming and tearing through places without warning. Water levels are rising and falling rapidly, destroying coastal cities. There are blizzards in arid climates and extreme heat waves in cold climates. The molecules in the atmosphere are reflecting odd radiation signatures and wavelengths, leading to the abnormal colours you see in the sky. It's as if Mother Nature has gone completely insane and has decided to wreak havoc on our planet!"

Giles wiped the sweat from his brow and let his head fall into his hands. "Every system in our world from as far back as we know has been built on the assumption that the foundations of time were stable. Time was solid and steady and dependable. Now, if the timeline is on the verge of collapsing—and all signs are pointing to that—everything we knew to be true will fade away to nothingness. We will be lost, we will know nothing, and we will be at the mercy of an unstable and volatile reality."

Suddenly, Giles straightened up, jumped from his chair, and rushed over to sit in front of one of the many computers. He mumbled something incoherent and started typing furiously. We followed and stood there watching him awkwardly for a while before we realized he was absorbed in his own world, oblivious of our continued presence. His fingers flew across his keyboard, and his eyes darted to different images rapidly popping up on his computer screen.

I patted his shoulder. "Thank you, Giles. We'll let you get back to it. I really appreciate all your hard work."

"Thanks, Mallick, love you too," he replied absentmindedly as he continued working.

I paused, and he slowly looked up and made eye contact, the realization of what he'd said just sinking in.

He rose to his feet, hitting his shin hard on the desk leg, and slipped past me while muttering, "If you'll excuse me, I need more caffeine."

Despite our grim circumstances, Tolli couldn't suppress his amusement. He looked at the ground and struggled to stop laughing. I tried to ignore him.

I couldn't help but compare Giles's report to William's speech on the logistics of time travel he'd given right before his death. He had considered that time travelling to the past could cause the timeline to implode in a multitude of different ways, and I believed he'd been right.

But it looked like time travel to the future wasn't any easier. Changing the future was what got us into this whole mess in the first place. If there ever were a time I needed William's help and advice, it was now.

Donahue interrupted my thoughts, "We can stop this. We have to."

October 1, 2059, 5:33 pm…

Donahue and Tolli left to grab supplies from the weapons vault while Wren and I walked back to her room.

She paused before going in and asked me, "Do you think my uncle intended for the orb to be used to power Tempus?"

"I have no idea what went on in William's head. Maybe. You were able to do it," I pointed out.

"It doesn't actually work without Amelia," she admitted and started pulling down the blueprints that covered her walls. "I've been wondering how Cyril ever got his hands on Uncle William's files."

I leaned over to pick up a table and straightened it against the wall, taking a moment to think. "I believe it must have happened sometime after the time machine's explosion, when William was killed. DAIR was in an uproar and scrambling to…uh, try to keep things quiet. They decided to downsize DTS immediately, diverting funds and resources to other areas until they could find a replacement for William. It must have been during that transition period that Cyril saw the opportunity to steal one of William's files without getting red-flagged. He took plans for a prototype that was never given clearance by DAIR to be built. William had called it an 'interdimensional transportation gateway apparatus' or ITGA."

"I like 'Whispers of Amelia' better," Wren remarked as she spread out her blueprints on the table. She bent over to collect all the tools that were scattered on the floor.

I nodded and knelt to help her. "I agree. I guess he just never thought of combining Amelia's design with Tempus's, but given more time, I'm sure he would have," I added sadly.

"Yeah." The tools clattered as she dropped them into her tool box. She picked at her lower lip before whispering, "I miss him."

"Me too." I pulled a chair up to the table for her and patted it. "He was a great man. He would have been so proud of you and Donahue."

She smiled slightly and brought her tool box to the table. I took a seat on a stool close by as she smoothed out the wrinkles in the blueprints and studied her work. I thought of how much she resembled her uncle when he was on the brink of solving a complex problem. Wren had the same intelligent, determined sparkle in her bright eyes as she leaned forward to study the papers laid out before her. She tapped her fingers together and pursed her lips.

Subconsciously, Wren rotated the weathered watch on her wrist. It looked vaguely familiar, but I didn't pay much attention to it. Just then, Donahue and Tolli noisily walked in behind us. I shifted in my seat to see them dressed head to toe in black combat gear. Tolli spun his laser taser around his finger.

"We got everything we need. The rest of the stuff is on the aircraft," Tolli announced and handed me a bag containing gear identical to theirs, a tactical belt, and a pistol.

"Except for one thing," Donahue added while adjusting his leather jacket. "Rob, do you know where the Circuit Toaster is?"

I narrowed my eyes at him. "I'm sorry, what?"

"It's a little white rectangle thing that disables Amelia's shield. It's about the size of my hand and has these pointy metal grills on the end."

"Is it experimental tech or something?" Tolli suggested, scratching the back of his head.

Wren joined in, not looking up as she started marking up her blueprints. "Doesn't Agent Jessie have it?"

"Why's it called a Circuit Toaster?" Tolli wondered and walked closer to peek over Wren's shoulder in curiosity.

Donahue shrugged and answered, "That's just what Jessie called it."

Something in my brain clicked, and I said, "I think I know what you're talking about. It's actually called a Concentrated Electron Disruptor or CED. They're not specifically used for disabling force fields. Quan said he could take care of that, but they can be used to disrupt and reroute electrical circuits safely. Is that what you used in the last loop? There should be one on the Osprey. I'll make sure I find it and keep it with me."

"Perfect." Donahue stepped over beside Wren, his eyes scanning her work. "Now, how are the blueprints looking, Wren? You designed all these?"

"The lightning trigger has got to go, but we still have to use the orb as a power source since there's no time to modify an existing system to accommodate anything else. I had a good look at the modifications you had made to Tempus III in the future and how you connected Amelia to it. I'm going to do all the same things, but I think we can connect Amelia to the bottom. When the portal opens beneath Tempus, gravity will be on our side, allowing us to fall through into the threads of time dimension. Now, the orb..."

Wren's voice trailed off as she pulled the mysterious orb out of her pocket and studied it closely in the palm of her hand. The eerie blue glow was visible between her metallic fingers. Donahue's attention also strayed from the blueprints to the orb.

She muttered under her breath, "If you're the cause of all this...no, you won't win. You have no control over me."

I stood up, but before I could react, Tolli butted in, "Uh, Red? What are you talking about? Who are you talking to?"

Wren shoved the orb back into her pocket, ignoring Tolli's queries, and finished her explanation. "If the orb is placed in the hole in the middle of Amelia's clawed disc, it would theoretically divert power directly to the machine."

"Brilliant," Donahue praised her, and a faint blush tinged her cheek that wasn't obscured by metal. I got the feeling they knew each other a lot more than they had let on. "With enough alterations to accommodate Amelia and the orb together along with additional stabilizers on the bottom, this could actually work."

Wren sighed, "These designs are barely more than concepts, but they'll have to do. We'll have to improvise as we go."

After a few moments of uncomfortable silence, Tolli asked Wren, "So, how long did it take to build the time machine in the other timeline? The one that worked?"

She hesitated before answering, "Eleven years."

Donahue glanced at his watch. "We have seven hours and two minutes. Give or take."

October 1, 2059, 6:31 pm...

Donahue, Wren, and I stood in the hall outside Wren's room. Donahue and I were about to leave for the hanger.

"See you soon, Rob." Wren wrapped her arms around me for a quick hug. "And thank you for believing me."

I had taken on the role of Wren's guardian after William had passed away two years ago. At times it had been difficult, but I did the best I could. I'd never had my own children, so Wren and Donahue were as close as it would ever be for me. Yet, as Wren squeezed me, we both knew that I was more than just a guardian. She was my girl. I realized I loved her as deeply as any father ever could, and I would do anything for her.

"I will always believe you," I said. And don't worry, Aquarius Deep is now considered an 'in-and-out' op, which means we get in and out as fast as possible, like we were never there. We'll be fine."

She broke away and addressed Donahue. "Please don't die again. And Cyril..."

"I won't."

Donahue pressed his lips together and shifted on the balls of his feet. The duffle bag slung on his shoulder swayed with each motion.

"That was my mistake. It won't happen again," he said resolutely.

She nodded.

He smiled at her. "If anyone in this entire world could build a time machine in a few hours, it would be you. I know you can do it."

"Thanks." Wren tucked a piece of hair behind her ear. "We're not going to fail this time."

Donahue shrugged, grasping her hand with a reassuring smile. "Third time's the charm?"

"We need to get moving," I reminded them.

The two had been inseparable during the past hour as they had worked on the blueprints and taken some of the time machine's engine apart.

"Goodbye, Alex. Please take care of yourself." She gave him a quick hug.

"I'll see you in about three hours. Give or take," he responded as he broke away, and we started down the hall. He looked back at her and adjusted the strap on his shoulder.

"She's a pretty special girl," I remarked, and Donahue avoided my gaze.

"Yep."

I bit my lip. "Do you want to talk about it?"

"Nope."

"All right then. If you change your mind, I'm always available." I pushed up my glasses and realized I was making him uncomfortable. "Tolli's waiting for us in the hanger. Let's pick up the pace."

Donahue nodded, then rubbed his forehead. "Can I ask you something?"

"Of course."

"Do you ever…have that voice in your head that just…" His voice trailed off as he tried to form the right words. "…Makes you so uncertain of everything?"

"You're having doubts. That's normal." However, my words didn't convince him.

Donahue slowly ran his fingers through his hair. "It's more than that. There are just some weird things it says…"

"Is it your voice or someone else's?"

He hesitated, a little surprised at my reaction. "I...I can't be sure exactly. I don't think it's mine...Do you think this is what Wren was talking about? About the orb?"

"I'm not sure. Before I asked you to pick Wren's lock, she and I had gone for a walk. I wanted to talk about the orb. I felt that it was affecting her somehow, and not in a good way. But, she's shown us that it has no power over her."

There were forces at play here that we couldn't fully comprehend. As director of DAWN and a close confidant of William Derecho, I knew more than I had let on, but not enough to connect all the dots.

"What do you mean?"

I raised an eyebrow at him. "The orb might be calling to you, but don't give in to its influence. Know that it has power, but also know that you can resist it. Focus on the mission, Donahue. We can figure out exactly what's going on after this crisis is averted."

After a moment, he answered quietly, "You're right."

≋ 6 HOURS and 28 MINUTES to TERMINUS TERRA

October 1, 2059, 7:02 pm…

I had made all the necessary arrangements with the ground crew before walking over to Donahue.

Tolli hauled Donahue's bulky duffle bag up the ramp leading to the back of the Osprey, dropping it with a thud at the top. "That's the last of the gear. We have everything we need, and the stealth crafts are ready for launch."

"All right," I spoke up, "I will take the Osprey, and you guys will fly the Sparrow. We'll touch down just after twenty-hundred hours and meet up with the rest of the team."

"Sounds good," Tolli replied as he sauntered down the ramp.

I adjusted my glasses and demanded, "Stay in touch and be careful."

The two young men nodded, and I watched as they walked over to the Sparrow. Tolli smiled and patted its metal hull with a thud. "Good to see you, little lady."

After years of being a part of many scientific breakthroughs, especially in advanced transportation technology, very little seemed to impress me. But a long time ago, like Tolli, I had gazed in admiration at the aircraft I was finally allowed access to after years of training. I missed those days.

I retracted the ramp and closed the cargo hatch before strolling through the fuselage to the Osprey's large cockpit. I took a seat and ran my hands along the flight controls, remembering my former days as a new DAWN recruit. I had been an exceptional pilot and wondered if I still had it in me.

"Well, let's find out," I mumbled to myself as I gazed out of the computerized windscreen.

A few minutes later, I was guiding the Osprey toward the open hanger door. As I approached the runway, I caught a glimpse of the Sparrow following close behind. I grinned, feeling the excitement of being a field agent once more. I made a mental note to talk to Mercier about changing some of DAWN's protocols after I returned. I had confided in her about the new plans, and even though she didn't fully approve, I convinced her to cover for me. For that, I owed her big time.

Halfway through the flight, I checked in with everyone. Wren had already removed Tempus II's lightning trigger and was starting to rewire the controls. Donahue and Tolli had gotten ahead of me since the Sparrow was more lightweight and aerodynamic, but they were experiencing spells of heavy turbulence as they neared the island.

As soon as I signed off with the team, my TetraScreen beeped loudly, indicating a call was coming through. I had forgotten that Mercier had given me another device, and I fumbled to shut it off, but it automatically synced to the speaker in the cockpit.

I clenched my jaw when I heard Director Li's voice. "Mallick, you better have a good reason why the Osprey and the Sparrow are missing from the hanger. Where are you?"

"Director Li," I said assertively, gripping the controls, "I don't have time to explain everything."

"And I don't have time to deal with this," she fired back. "Turn around."

"I'll be back soon," I lied. "I know what I'm doing. Operation Aquarius Deep is compromised, so I've had to revise the plan. You're just going to have to trust me on this one."

"Mallick, you're acting irrationally." Director Li commanded, "I demand an explanation."

I didn't reply.

"Mallick!" She yelled, her voice escalating through the speaker. "Are you still there? Can you hear me? Mallick!"

As soon as I cut off the connection, I knew I would have a lot of questions to answer when I got back.

October 1, 2059, 8:14 pm...

The sun had dipped into the sea, but wisps of gold still lingered on the horizon. After activating the invisibility cloak, I landed the Osprey in the clearing on Cyril's island, out of view from the watchtowers. As soon as the stealth craft came to a halt, a voice burst through the speaker in the cockpit, crackling with static.

"Does anybody copy?" Agent Cassandra Viola's voice rang clearer than the rest of the other agents.

"I read you," I replied. "Get your team to the rendezvous point immediately."

I didn't want to say anything more since the channel wasn't secure.

"Roger. Over and out."

Donahue's voice came through my earpiece, "Rob, stay put. Tolli and I are heading your way. We landed on the other side of the clearing. See you soon."

"Affirmative."

I slipped the box of new earpieces into my pocket and took the CED or "Circuit Toaster" out of a compartment in the wall. I grabbed my combat jacket and waited for my team to assemble.

"Agent Mallick, what's going on?" Viola questioned as she and Agent Adeline Jessie approached the Osprey.

I stood on the ramp with Donahue and Tolli, who had arrived a few minutes after I landed. Behind Jessie and Viola, Agent Keemo Nhu and his partner, Agent Ben Hammerschlag, appeared at the edge of the clearing, side by side. The two middle-aged agents, who made up half the group we called "the Vets," couldn't have looked more different from each other. Nhu was short and lean with a round face and large eyes. His black hair was tied back in a loose ponytail that bounced as he scurried to keep up with Hammerschlag's long strides. In contrast, Hammerschlag was broad-shouldered and tall. While his white-blonde buzz cut seemed to glow in the dark, his deep-set eyes were hidden in shadow.

Jessie removed a large twig from her long braid and added, "We've lost all contact with the control centre."

"I know." I could tell these agents had been under a lot of stress in the last few hours. "We've had a change of plans. I'll be running Aquarius Deep from the ground, and our prime objective remains the same: to retrieve Amelia. A traitor's been discovered within DAWN, which is why it was necessary to make last-minute changes. These adjustments have now left only the seven of us to ensure the success of this op."

"Seven? What about Quan?" Nhu asked.

"Kyler Quan is the double agent."

A moment of silence passed through the group as the shocking information settled in.

Nhu retied his dark ponytail and blinked hard a few times. "Well, are we gonna take him out?"

Hammerschlag stepped forward, nudging his friend aside, and cracked his knuckles. "You better let me handle him, Grandpa."

"Watch it, Hammer. I'm only five years older than you," Nhu retorted, "and I can still dance circles around you."

Viola's cheeks flushed as she grumbled, "I'll make that snake wish he'd never been born."

"Vee versus Quan. Man, I'd buy a ticket to that showdown!" Tolli remarked, grinning.

"That won't be necessary," I cut in. "Eliminating Quan is not the priority here." I held up my hand so no one would interrupt me again and instructed, "Donahue, Viola, Tolli, you'll come with me to the watchtower on the northwest corner. Nhu, Jessie, Hammerschlag, each of you takes one of the other three watchtowers. On my mark, we attack at the same time."

The expressions on their faces had grown serious.

"After all four watchtowers are secure, Nhu and Jessie will head back to the Sparrow, and Hammerschlag to the Osprey. The rest of us will use a grappling hook to zip-line to the dome on the top floor. We'll drop through the top, disable Amelia's shield, and prepare her for transport. We'll have to move fast. Best-case scenario: the room will be empty, and we'll be in and out in no time.

"Meanwhile, Nhu and Jessie will fly the Sparrow above the dome and send down a rope. Tolli and Viola will be responsible for attaching Amelia's control box to the rope and getting it up to the Sparrow. Donahue and I will cover them. We'll have to time this perfectly down to the second." I looked at Hammerschlag. "Hammerschlag, have the Osprey ready for a quick extraction through the roof for the four of us."

"You got it, Sir."

"Once Amelia is on the Sparrow, Nhu and Jessie, head straight back to headquarters. Don't wait for us, especially if we're delayed. It's crucial that Amelia gets to…Room T-117. Everyone else, board the Osprey, and we go home. Clear?"

The group of agents nodded. I took the box of bronze earpieces out of my jacket pocket. "Recon team, use these. Throw away your old ones; they've been compromised. Make sure to stay in contact."

"We're racing against the clock on this one," Donahue emphasized as the four agents replaced their earpieces.

Tolli pointed his thumbs at himself. "Don't worry, 'Speedy' is my middle name."

His response was met with a few groans and eye rolls as Donahue glared at him.

"Grab your gear," I ordered. "Let's move out."

4 HOURS and 43 MINUTES to TERMINUS TERRA

October 1, 2059, 8:47 pm...

Our targeted watchtower's beam of light swept by us, and Viola, Tolli, Donahue, and I ducked into the brush until it passed over. The four watchtowers stood a whole story taller than the highest part of the stone building. I studied it in the dim light; a cylindrical pod, encircled by tinted glass, sat on top of a thinner base.

"In position," Jessie reported through my earpiece.

"Hammer in position," Hammerschlag added quickly.

Nhu jumped in, "Waiting for the signal."

"All right, let's roll," I responded as my heart rate sped up. "Go, go, go!"

Viola signalled for us to stay and crept around closer to the entrance at the base. A lone guard stood outside the door with his rifle held diagonally across his chest. He whistled to himself, rocking on the balls of his feet. Tolli tried to keep the large duffle bag he carried from making noise as the supplies inside shifted; however, the guard heard and swept his rifle out in front of him.

"Who's there?"

In the blink of an eye, Viola knocked the rifle out of his grasp and kicked him in the chin. He slumped to the ground, unconscious. The three of us ran directly to the door and followed Viola as she climbed the spiral stone staircase to the top of the tower. We neutralized the two guards monitoring the security camera feeds as well as the one controlling the tower's spotlight.

I relayed, "Watchtower One is secure."

We waited for a few stressful minutes before we heard Jessie's voice. "Watchtower Two secure."

"Copy that. Watchtower Three secure. Just waiting for Grandpa," Hammerschlag teased.

Nervous silence ensued until we heard Nhu, out of breath, gasp, "Stop calling me that. Watchtower Four secure, heading to the Sparrow now."

Tolli dropped his duffle bag and unzipped it. He retrieved a small laser glass cutter to use on the tower window. Once he'd outlined a large rectangle, Donahue and Viola used dual suction cups from the bag to carefully remove the glass.

"All right, who has the best shot?" Tolli wondered out loud as he took out the harnesses and threw one to each of us.

"Probably Vee from what I've heard," Donahue answered as he slipped on his harness.

Viola smiled. "Is that even a question? Donahue, nice to meet you, by the way."

I pulled out the grappling gun from the bag and handed it to her as Tolli collected the tools. She approached the open window, the draft catching her dark hair and blowing it across her face. She took a second to slow her breathing, aimed, and then fired. The grips on the flower-shaped tip embedded into the stone right below the bottom panels of the dome, and Viola gave the rope a sharp tug to ensure it was secure.

She wrapped the rope around a metal beam above the window and fastened it firmly before jamming the gun through the railing at the top of the stairs. "Now, who's first?"

"Me!" Tolli responded, thrilled at the prospect of jumping out of a window six stories up. "I mean…me! I'll go first. I mean, whatever you think, Mallick."

I signalled for him to go ahead. Tolli eagerly slung the duffle bag back across his shoulder and attached his harness to the line before leaping out.

Donahue peeked out of the window at the ground.

"It's pretty high," he remarked, his voice faltering a little at the end before he followed his partner on the zip line.

Viola saluted me before she jumped out and disappeared into the darkness.

I went last, clenching my jaw. "I'm getting too old for this," I whispered to myself.

I took a deep breath before stepping out the window into thin air. The wind tugged at my clothes as I slid down the rope. In that moment, I felt alive, free from the stress of the crazy events of the day. I hadn't felt adrenaline pump through my veins like this for many years.

I squeezed the handbrakes as I approached the end of the line. Tolli was already cutting through a glass panel with the laser glass cutter. The rest of us attached the dual suction cups to the sides and lifted it together. Once the whole thing was removed, Tolli retrieved a coil of rope from his bag, tied it to the end of the grappling hook, and then threw the other end over the edge. I couldn't help but feel a strong sense of pride as I watched my team work without a trace of fear or hesitancy. It felt good to see everything firsthand, instead of directing them from headquarters.

"Use this to disable the shield. Tolli's familiar with it." I handed Viola the Circuit Toaster. Curious, she ran a thumb down the side of the white rectangular contraption.

Tolli gestured to Viola to go. "Ladies first."

She gave him a playful shove before sliding down the rope into Amelia's room. One by one, the rest of us descended. It was dark, but Amelia's glowing pink shield provided enough light for us to see.

As soon as my boots hit the floor, I heard Donahue's voice echo through my earpiece, "We're in, guys."

"Nhu, Jessie, bring the Sparrow to the top of the dome," I ordered. "We'll be ready in a few minutes."

"Roger that."

The four of us crept toward Amelia, and I checked in with the Osprey, "Hammerschlag?"

"In position, sir."

Just as everything seemed to be going according to plan, a gravelly voice came from behind us. "Don't move. Drop your weapons."

I turned around to see a gray-haired man. His face was half-hidden by an unkempt beard.

Xavi Khanna.

The older man's dark features clearly resembled Donahue's. They shared the same thin lips, hooked nose, and wavy hair that fell into their eyes. Donahue's bright-blue eyes were highlighted even more in contrast to his father's dark ones. Viola and Tolli quickly drew their laser tasers and trained them on Xavi. I slowly moved my hand toward the gun on my belt as my eyes locked onto Xavi's.

"No!" Donahue blurted and stepped forward with his hands raised. "Don't shoot!"

Xavi was only distracted for a split second before his focus and pistol were directed back toward me. Suspicious recognition shone in his eyes. "You...you're DAWN's director."

"I am," I admitted.

"Baba," Donahue choked out, and the older man's gaze flicked to him. "Baba, it's me, Alex."

"Alex?" Xavi blinked rapidly in disbelief. "No, my son is dead." His eyes narrowed cynically, and he gestured at me with his gun. "This man is responsible for his death. Tell your agents to drop their weapons, or I'll shoot. You're not going anywhere with that machine."

"No." I raised my hands defensively and shook my head. "Xavi, you were lied to. This is your son. This is Alex."

Donahue walked toward his father, keeping his arms up. As Xavi studied his son's face, his fierce expression gave way to astonishment. Tears welled up and glistened in his eyes. "How can this be? Your eyes...I'd recognize them anywhere. My boy."

Donahue rushed forward and pulled his father into a tight hug. I relaxed slightly and signalled to Viola and Tolli to continue.

"I don't understand. I thought I lost you," Xavi whispered hoarsely, oblivious to what was going on around him.

Vee tossed the Circuit Toaster to Tolli, and he jabbed it into the base of the shield's generator to disable it. The shield glitched and spluttered before shutting off completely. Vee retrieved heavy-duty elastics from a small pack attached to her waist. They worked quickly and efficiently to secure them around Amelia, and I trusted they had it under control.

I turned my attention back to Xavi and Donahue.

Xavi reluctantly released his son and swallowed hard. "Cyril found me somehow and told me DAWN had executed my family on Mallick's orders. You and your mother were the only two people I had left in this world, and you were stolen from me. Cyril offered me a chance to join him in his fight against DAIR, so I poured myself into building Whispers of Amelia…and, I think, this machine is why you're here, right?"

I faintly heard the Sparrow's engine above the dome, and a rope was lowered through the hole in the roof. Viola and Tolli quickly attached Amelia to the metal fastener and gave Nhu the okay to start hauling it up. Xavi's gaze wandered to them for only a moment, but he didn't react.

Xavi's voice cracked as he stuttered, "I'm so sorry…I-I didn't know."

"Donahue, Mallick," Tolli called out as Amelia disappeared out of sight. "It's time."

"It's not your fault, Baba." Donahue's voice was barely audible as he tried to keep his tears at bay. "Come with us."

Donahue and Xavi's gaze locked for a few long, uninterrupted seconds; a thousand words were left unsaid.

"No, Alex, I can't. I need to make sure you get out of here." Xavi looked toward the door. "Go, they'll be here any second now."

I pulled Donahue by his arm, and he complied with a blank expression. Hammerschlag had already dropped the thick extraction rope equipped with four attachment devices eight feet apart to buckle our harnesses into.

As Tolli fastened Donahue's harness, I nodded thanks to the older man. "Xavi, I…I don't know what to say to you. I'm sorry."

"Don't be. You brought my son to me." He smiled and gestured for me to go.

I turned to leave. Out of the corner of my eye, the silhouette of a man distinguishable by his tall mohawk burst into the room. He was out of breath.

"Mallick!"

"Quan, you traitor." The words escaped my mouth as my anger erupted without warning.

He pressed his lips together and growled, "You're not going anywhere, Mallick."

Quan whipped out his pistol and fired as I moved toward the others. They covered me, forcing him to dive behind some steel barrels at the edge of the room. Sweat dripped down the back of my neck as I quickly clipped myself onto the last section of the rope.

"Now, Hammer!" I shouted into my earpiece.

I gripped the rope tightly as we moved upward. I twisted my body around, so I could aim my gun at Quan, but hesitated to pull the trigger as Xavi stood directly in the line of fire.

"What are you standing there for, Khanna?" Quan yelled at Xavi, who hadn't moved. "Help me!"

The other three passed through the gap in the roof. I was almost to safety when bullets started whizzing by me, shattering the glass above my head. Xavi launched himself into Quan, knocking him to the ground.

I felt nothing. Then I felt everything.

As soon as I was lifted into the cool night air, I thought I had smashed my left arm against the metal skeleton of the glass dome. My shoulder seared with pain like it had been lit on fire, and I slumped back in my harness, unable to hold on. I fought to keep conscious as I spun in dizzying circles on the extraction rope.

My brain grew foggy as Tolli and Donahue helped me into the belly of the Osprey. Thunder boomed in the distance; a storm was brewing.

4 HOURS and 7 MINUTES to TERMINUS TERRA

October 1, 2059, 9:23 pm…

I'm fine, I'm fine! It just grazed me," I insisted for the tenth time. "I'll live."

Donahue sat beside me, inspecting the bullet wound in my shoulder. "Rob, you were *shot*. I wouldn't call that a graze, but I think you'll be all right."

Donahue assisted me in wrapping it with some bandages from the first aid kit onboard the Osprey. The bleeding slowed as the wound was compressed, but I added another layer for good measure and gingerly slipped my jacket back on. The hum of the aircraft filled our ears as our conversation trailed off. I held my throbbing arm against my torso and lay down on the vacant seat beside me as the last of my adrenaline wore off. I wasn't sure how much help I would be to them now, but I fully trusted in the competence of my team.

As soon as I began to relax, the stealth craft rattled violently as a burst of light exploded near the window on the opposite side of me.

I jolted up in my seat. "Hammer! What's going on?"

"Sir, we've got company. Engine One is down. I just activated the outer shield."

Donahue and I exchanged concerned glances and strained to look out the window into the night sky.

"I don't see—" Tolli was interrupted by a loud whine directly above us.

"SuperNovas," Viola breathed out as she squinted to make out distant shadows outside. "I've heard of them. They must be Cyril's. They're tiny and nearly impossible to track, but the damage they can inflict is enough to take out any aircraft. Even ours."

"Those are definitely SuperNovas," Hammerschlag confirmed as he rolled right. "Our invisibility cloak is useless if they've already found us. I'm turning it off to redirect power to the outer shield."

I braced myself against my seat as another brilliant explosion lit up the windows. The whole aircraft shuddered, triggering a series of blinking warnings. Viola and Tolli rushed toward the cockpit as I struggled to lift myself up.

"Stay in your seat, Rob. We can handle this," Donahue insisted, but the expression on his face revealed that he already knew I would never do that.

He held out his hand. I stood up, put my arm around Donahue's shoulder, and leaned on him. He had no choice but to help me, and, together, we stumbled into the cockpit.

I addressed our pilot. "Hammerschlag, how much ammo did we stock?" When he didn't answer, I finished, "Well, we're about to find out. Everyone, take a station."

Donahue, Tolli, and Viola scattered off to different parts of the Osprey. A drop of sweat slid down Hammerschlag's temples as he checked the radar scanners. Just as I slipped into the seat beside him, keeping my injured arm close to my chest, the outer shield crackled and lit up as it was bombarded with a series of explosives. I caught a glimpse of the deadly stealth crafts climbing vertically, then branching off from one another and vanishing from sight.

"Mallick, what's going on back there?" Jessie asked through the comms.

"We're under attack," I responded. "SuperNovas."

"We're turning around," Nhu insisted, "We can help."

"Negative. Get the package to the facility and deliver it to Room T-117," I commanded. "We can take care of ourselves."

The entire aircraft rattled, then jerked to one side as the enemy fired above us, their black shapes barely visible as they retreated. Outside the windscreen, red, pink, and purple sparks crackled, indicating the outer shield was failing.

"Anything on the radar?" Donahue questioned.

I bit my lip, glancing at the radar. "No, it's clean—wait, target single SuperNova, six o'clock."

"Targeted," Viola, Donahue, and Tolli confirmed.

"Cleared to engage," I yelled into the comms.

I felt a steady series of thuds as our counterattack was launched into the darkness. A shadow passed above us. I stared up at the flat, aerodynamic "V" shape of the black SuperNova with one side enveloped in flames.

"Splash one," Tolli reported as the jet spiralled toward the depths of the South Seas.

One swooped up from underneath the Osprey, and another flew straight toward us, firing without mercy. Hammerschlag banked left, causing everything to tumble and crash. The aircraft shuddered, and red and orange lights flashed on the cockpit's computerized windscreen. The radar screen went blank, no longer able to locate the invisible, deadly pests.

"Engine Two is down, and the shield is toast," Hammerschlag shouted. "I don't know how many more hits we can take, Mallick."

There was a slight quiver in Jessie's voice coming through the comms. "Are you sure you don't want us to turn back, sir?"

"Stay on course. Don't ask me again."

A whine came from outside, barely audible over the hum of the Osprey's engines. A jet spiralled through the air as it dove toward us. Hammerschlag rolled right to quickly manoeuvre out of the line of fire, and the SuperNova climbed upward, slicing through the air.

Over the comms, Tolli's rushed words betrayed his frustration. "This isn't working, sir."

Hammerschlag looked at me. "What do we do?"

I firmly addressed my team, "We need something quick that takes them all down at the same time. This isn't even about us getting away from them. They can't get to the facility. What about some sort of mass explosion?"

Viola suggested, "Can we use the Circuit Toaster? I still have it in my pocket."

Tolli jumped in, "What if we could hook up the Circuit Toaster to one of the Osprey's power sources to create a gigantic Electro-Magnetic Pulse jammer? A large-scale EMP blast would create a magnetic field that would interfere with all functioning electrical systems within its scope. Do we have any other ideas?"

Donahue commented, "Nope. Let's use the secondary auxiliary power unit."

Hammerschlag exhaled sharply and pressed his lips together. "If all electrical systems within a certain radius shut down, that includes us."

I responded, "I'm aware of that, but we have to ensure Cyril doesn't get Amelia back anytime soon. IWS has a reboot program..."

Another massive hit rocked the Osprey, but this time without any protection from the shield. Hammerschlag strained to straighten the aircraft.

"We've lost Engine Three," Hammerschlag grunted and wiped his forehead with his sleeve. "That leaves one left. We're on our last leg, and there's still at least three SuperNovas out there."

He peered below at the endless, dark waves. "If the Osprey activates the reboot, it will take twenty seconds...twenty seconds of free fall."

"I'm good with twenty seconds. All right, let's go! Hammer, buy us as much time as you can."

I switched on the channel to the back to hear Tolli, Viola, and Donahue's hurried footsteps in the fuselage. They rushed to the control panel connected to the secondary auxiliary power unit. It only took Tolli a few seconds to wire the Circuit Toaster to it.

"We're good to go, Mallick," Tolli yelled.

I interrupted, "Everyone, brace yourselves. Activate the EMP now, Donahue."

Donahue announced, "The EMP is live in three...two...one."

Darkness enveloped us as the electric shock wave surged and dissipated. We glided for a moment before the nose of the stealth craft slowly dipped down. My heart leapt into my throat, and I felt weightless in my seat as we plummeted down. The seat straps cut into my shoulder, and I bit my lip to keep from crying out in pain.

"Fifteen seconds to reboot," Hammerschlag reported. "Altitude twenty thousand feet."

I looked out the windscreen to see shadows falling out of the starry sky.

"Ten seconds. Fifteen thousand feet."

"Mallick!" Viola shouted, but her voice was almost drowned out by the howling wind outside.

Tolli added, "We're not going to make it!"

"Five seconds." Hammerschlag swallowed hard. "Ten thousand feet." His forehead creased as he counted, "Three, two, one…"

We were seconds away from colliding with the white-capped waves below. Impact would mean certain death.

"Uh…" Hammerschlag clutched his armrests.

"Come on." I gritted my teeth.

The power re-engaged, and Hammerschlag pulled the stick back hard, causing us to slam back down against our seats. We accelerated upward.

One by one, the SuperNovas disappeared into the darkness for the last time, swallowed up by the water below.

"Splash two. Splash three. Splash four."

October 1, 2059, 10:03 pm...

"Rob, we'll get you to the infirmary as soon as we land," Donahue told me.

We'd already had this conversation multiple times during the flight, and this would be the final time as we were about to arrive at the facility in a few minutes.

"We have far more important matters at hand. I'll get medical attention later," I reasoned, then lied, "Besides, I can barely feel it."

"Because you're in shock," Tolli suggested, leaning forward on his seat directly across from me.

"I'm not in shock. I'll be okay."

I turned away from him as Jessie's voice came through my earpiece, "We just touched down. Preparing to unload the package now."

I nodded. "Good."

"We'll arrive shortly," Hammerschlag called out from the cockpit. "We lost quite a bit of time."

Donahue mumbled into his earpiece, "We'll see you soon, Wren."

I made eye contact with him, and his eyes darted to my arm. I hardened my gaze and firmly told him, "Do not tell her."

Immediately after the Osprey came to a halt inside the hanger, Tolli, Donahue, and I hurried out, leaving Hammerschlag to complete the after-landing procedures. Nhu and Jessie were waiting for us.

"Where are you guys going?" Jessie asked. "We delivered the package to the girl in Room T-117. Are you going to tell us what's going on, Mallick?"

"It's complicated."

Everything from the last couple of hours had blurred together, and I hadn't put much thought into what I had to do when we got back. It was uncharacteristic of me to be unprepared, making me wonder if my injury might have affected me more than I thought.

I hastily explained, "But I need you to do something for me right away. I need you guys to find Director Li and tell her Aquarius Deep was a success. Try to answer any questions she has, but tell her I will explain everything as soon as I can. I just need a few more hours."

Tolli and I left Nhu and Jessie without waiting for them to respond and rushed to catch up with Donahue, who had already burst through the large swinging doors. I glanced back to see Viola following us.

"Viola, what are you doing?"

She matched her stride with ours as we sped through corridors, weaving through agents and scientists. "You guys are acting strange. I want to know what's going on."

"No—"

Tolli interjected, "We can trust her, Mallick. Plus, we could use her help."

There wasn't time to argue, so I just sighed. Viola smiled gratefully at Tolli, and we climbed the flight of stairs up to Wren's room.

At the top, Donahue called over his shoulder, "C'mon, Wren's room is just over here!"

Viola stopped in her tracks. "Wait, did you say..."

Before she could finish, Wren met us just outside of her room. "Hey, guys. Glad you're back. Everyone's talking about how you—" Her emerald-green eyes flicked to Viola, and her voice faltered, "Cass?"

"Wren?" Viola cried, and her eyes widened with surprise. She steadied herself against the wall.

Wren rushed over to her and hugged her tightly. "Yeah, it's me."

Viola was one of my most composed, stoic agents, so I wasn't expecting her to break down sobbing. I glanced at Tolli and Donahue; they seemed to be as thrown off as I was. Distracted, I went to slip my hands in my pockets, but the motion sent a wave of agony emanating from my shoulder. For a moment, all my strength drained from my body, and I bit down on my tongue to keep from yelling out.

"Your face...your arm," Viola whispered as she released Wren. She reached out and touched the metal on her forearm.

Wren nodded. "The accident...I didn't die."

I couldn't make the connection to what these girls were alluding to. *How many people did Wren know in this facility? How much didn't I know?*

"I don't understand..." Viola's voice trailed off.

"I know," Wren responded, studying Viola's face. "Long story. I don't even know where to begin."

"Wren," Donahue interrupted and gestured to his watch.

"Right. Cass, I'm sorry. I can explain everything after we break the time loop."

"Wait, what did you say?" Viola's brow wrinkled, unable to process the absurdity of Wren's statement.

I didn't blame her since I had been in the same position a few hours earlier.

"Basically, we're stuck in a time loop, and Alex and I are the only ones aware of it. The only way we think we can break everyone out of it is to travel to the future in a time machine," Wren summarized and gestured to Tempus's metal hull that was propped up on cement blocks in her room. "Amelia is the key for this to work. That's why we had to get it back here."

"I can't believe this...I just can't believe today," Viola muttered, shaking her head.

Wren squeezed her friend's hand. "Cass, I need you to trust me on this."

Viola took a moment, and then nodded. "At this point, what choice do I have?"

"Okay, so you said that we needed to attach Amelia to the bottom of Tempus…" Donahue paused and looked back over his shoulder to give Wren a puzzled look. "What number are we on?"

"I think numbers are irrelevant now," Wren answered as the rest of us followed him inside. "Let's just call it Tempus…uh…DAWN?"

"Tempus *Aurora*. Perfect." Donahue smiled faintly. "We need to attach Amelia's disc to Tempus Aurora." He stepped toward Amelia, which was parked beside the time machine, and turned to Tolli. "Tolli, knife."

Tolli grinned and tossed him his pocket knife, and Donahue got to work dissecting Amelia's rubber tubing. Bundles of colourful wires tumbled out. Tolli motioned for Viola to help him disassemble the control box. A green glow from inside it reflected off his face as he studied the contraption closely. In a daze, Viola glanced at Wren before wandering over to Tolli.

Wren picked up a flash welder and was about to slip underneath Tempus Aurora when she noticed me clutching my left arm. I winced as I shifted my jacket sleeve, trying to hide my reaction.

"Rob, is something wrong?"

I dismissed the question swiftly. "Ah, no, I'm just sore. Keep going."

She looked at me suspiciously, but turned her attention back to the time machine. Once I was out of her sight, I leaned weakly against a table. I gritted my teeth and focused on my breathing as a wave of nausea passed over me.

"Hey, Rob, can you pass me those wire clippers?" Wren questioned and peeked out from under Tempus Aurora.

Her large emerald-coloured eyes stared up at me expectantly. I forced a smile and nodded, pushing myself off the table. I grabbed the wire clippers that had been tossed onto a nearby stool.

The choice was clear; I needed to help the people I loved most, so I ignored the increasing pain in my arm.

19 MINUTES
to TERMINUS TERRA

October 2, 2059, 1:11 am...

"**A**re you done with that yet? I thought your middle name was 'Speedy,'" Viola teased.

"Oh, I was just kidding." Tolli placed a small screwdriver between his teeth as he finished piecing together wires in a side panel. "It's actually...um...'Rockstar.'"

I couldn't help but smile at Tolli's look of satisfaction when he got a laugh out of her.

The next few hours consisted of frustrated outbursts, hurried and confusing explanations, and a variety of tools being strewn about as we finished merging Amelia's disc to the bottom of Tempus Aurora. Tolli and Donahue tackled the wiring underneath while Wren finished programming the controls. Viola and I helped where we could, but we were clearly out of our element. I tried my best to catch her up on everything that Donahue and Wren had explained to me about our predicament as well as how Wren had ended up in our facility.

My vision blurred as Tolli and I held metal beams in place while Wren finished securing them with her small flash welder. I tried to blink away the foggy sensation in my brain by focusing on the metal tubing surrounding the disc like a spider web.

After we had finished, Wren absentmindedly glanced at the broken watch on her wrist and realized it was unhelpful. "Alex, how long until the loop resets?"

"Approximately eighteen minutes. It was zero-one-thirty hours when Amelia exploded in the first two loops."

Tolli wiped the sweat from his brow. "You're cutting it real close, guys."

He slapped the metal side of the pyramid hull, but as soon as he did, Tempus Aurora's lights switched on by themselves while the fluorescent lights on the ceiling sparked and flickered off. Tolli jumped back.

The time machine rose a few inches off the ground, and Wren stepped closer to it. Through the small round windows on the sides, the control console emitted an eerie blue-green glow. It hovered for a minute before the whole thing shut off and smashed back onto the concrete blocks it had been propped up on.

My head throbbed, and the floor seemed to tilt. I struggled to keep my balance in the darkness and stumbled forward. I crashed into a table, its legs screeching as it scraped against the ground. I barely felt the collision as the pain in my shoulder reignited, exploding in a sensation I hadn't ever experienced before. I felt something warm drip down my arm, and the strength drained from my legs. My knees buckled from under me, and I suddenly found myself sprawled on the floor, the cold concrete pressing against the side of my face.

"Rob?" Donahue choked out as the backup generators kicked in, and the lights blinked sporadically before switching on again.

He rushed over to me. Every breath brought another wave of agony, and my throat constricted, making breathing nearly impossible. Coughing, I touched my shoulder and glanced at my hand; it was covered in dark-red liquid.

"Rob!" Wren screamed, then covered her mouth.

Donahue gently pulled my jacket down past the bandage, and I let out a strangled cry. He gasped as my face twisted in pain.

I exhaled, "What's wrong?"

"Vee, Tolli, go get a doctor," Donahue shouted. "Now!"

I looked down to see the blood-stained bandage. Underneath it, bulging green veins ran down my forearm from the wound. Wren dropped to her knees beside me; her eyes were wide and unblinking.

Tolli and Viola dashed toward the door. As Tolli disappeared,

Viola called out over her shoulder, "We'll take care of Mallick. Break the time loop. You two need to get out of here."

Donahue helped me roll onto my side and propped my head up on his lap. I dug my nails into my palm and clenched my jaw until I thought my teeth would break.

Donahue frowned. "It looks like that bullet was laced with something."

I struggled to hear him as a ringing sound grew steadily in my ears.

"I don't know. I've never seen anything like..." I strained to read the time on Donahue's watch. "It doesn't matter right now. Viola is right. You guys need to go."

As each second passed, I could feel my remaining strength leaving my body, and dark spots started flickering across my vision. I looked up at Wren and Donahue. "I love you both. You know that, right?"

Making sure that they knew I loved them was the most important thing I could think of; in fact, it was the only thing that really mattered to me in these last few moments.

Donahue nodded slightly as he stared at me and tried to say something, but he couldn't find the words. Wren's lip quivered, and tears spilled down her face.

She gripped my hand in her metallic ones and cried, "Rob, don't talk like that. You're not leaving us. You're going to be okay."

"Wren..." Donahue's voice trailed off.

"There's so much more I need to tell you...but there's no time," I weakly breathed out.

A fleeting look of confusion passed over Wren's face, but it quickly shifted back into fear.

The darkness that had lingered at the edge of my vision began to seep in and merge with the dancing spots. They began to cloud my eyesight, and I couldn't fight back any longer. I couldn't help them anymore.

I needed to go. I needed to go, so they could keep going.

"Go."

PART FIVE
WREN DERECHO

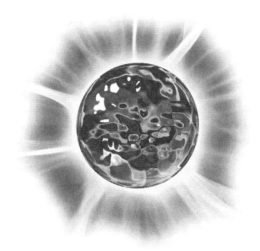

3 MINUTES to TERMINUS TERRA

October 2, 2059, 1:27 am...

I shook Rob forcefully, desperately refusing to let him go. The skin around his wound had taken on a sickly gray hue. His glasses fell from his face, and his brown eyes stared right through me.

"Wake up, Rob." My sobs were muffled as I buried my face into his chest.

Dad. Mom. Uncle William. And now Rob. Everyone I had called family was gone. They had all been taken from me.

Tears blurred my vision as Alex gently laid Rob on the ground and stood up. He tried to pull me away from Rob's stone-still body. I ripped my arm out of his grasp, wanting to scream at him, but I couldn't breathe. I wanted to scream at Rob to get up. To stop pretending. To stop lying there, lifeless. I didn't understand how this could happen, and my shock mixed with rage turned into pure hysteria.

Alex, once again, yanked on my arm. "Wren, we have to go."

"We can't just leave him here. How can you just stand there?" Angry tears streamed down my face, and my voice went up an octave. "How could you let this happen?"

"We're out of time." Alex let go of me and walked back toward Tempus Aurora, his fists clenched at his sides. "It's happening again. This timeline is going to fade away just like the others. If we don't leave, everyone else in this world will die. We have to do what Rob wanted. I didn't let it happen, Wren. He refused medical treatment because he thought what we were doing was more important. Nobody could have known the bullet was laced with something."

He paused and tried to blink away the tears in his eyes. He looked back at me and pleaded, "He wanted us to keep going. We have to go."

Begrudgingly, I wiped my face on my sleeve even as the tears continued to flow, reluctant to accept that there wasn't even time to grieve. I quickly retrieved the sheet from my bed and leaned over to kiss Rob on the cheek. My chin trembled as I tried to stop crying.

Carefully, I draped the sheet over his body and whispered, "Goodbye."

Heartbroken, but still determined, I looked up at Alex through tear-filled eyes and nodded. "I'm ready."

My concentration broke as an empty glass on one of the tables began to rattle slightly. As if on cue, tremors vibrated the floor beneath our feet. I felt the orb in my pocket grow increasingly warmer against my leg. I fished it out; the orb was glowing and radiating heat. I slipped underneath Tempus Aurora to stick the power source into the centre of the disc.

Alex swung open the time machine's door and took a seat at the control desk. I leapt in after him and sealed the door behind me. As Alex's fingers flew across the digital controls, the entire machine began to shudder.

My breath caught in my throat. "No, no, no. The anomalies couldn't have reached us yet."

Suddenly, Alex's hands froze over top of the controls. He pressed his temples and moaned, "Stop it. Stop talking."

"What?" I retorted, offended.

"Nothing. It's nothing." Alex shook his head, leaving me very confused. "Do you feel like all the loops are fusing together or something? It all seems to be one jumbled mess...and the voice..."

I narrowed my eyes. "Are you okay?"

He stared at me and didn't answer. For a second, I had an eerie feeling in my gut as his blue eyes locked with mine; however, the urgency of the moment took over. The odd exchange was soon forgotten as Alex turned back to the screen.

He quickly resumed programming and tapped on the control console to activate the thrusters. As we hovered above the ground, I strained to look out of the round windows at the dark waves rippling throughout the floor of my room.

"It works," I breathed out as a black hole slowly opened up and churned in a shadowy spiral storm underneath us.

Alex grabbed my metal hand in his, a worried expression on his face, as he strained to look out the window.

"I'm so glad I'm not doing this alone," I whispered.

He turned back to me and smiled. "Me too."

Just as we were preparing to descend into the threads of time, a burst of energy exploded beneath Tempus Aurora, propelling it upward a few feet. I grabbed onto the back of the seat and braced myself against the slanted walls. I glanced out the window and saw the portal dissipating. The machine crashed back down against the concrete with a clang that reverberated through my bones, and my head slammed against the side.

All the lights went out, leaving the two of us in pitch-black darkness.

≋ TERMINUS TERRA ACTIVATED

October 2, 2059, 1:31 am...

"What? What happened?" Alex groaned and gingerly touched his split lip. Red emergency lights now throbbed in the darkness. "I don't think it worked. What do we do now?"

"I-I don't know," I stuttered, rubbing the back of my head. The impact had caused me to fall onto my knees. I got to my feet and looked around in confusion. My voice rose, "It should have worked! Amelia is supposed to make it work! Why didn't it work? What time is it?"

"It's 1:31."

"So, we're out of the time loop? We were able to skip ahead one minute?"

Alex pressed the heels of his hands into his eyes and sighed, "I don't know. But, we can't stay here, Wren. The tremors are getting worse."

I gasped, "The timeline...it's going to collapse. We're too late." I recalled my last adventure and how the whole city of Ashborne crumbled as my friends and I had rushed back to Tempus III to escape being erased from existence. They had died in that reality so I could make it back. "Cass and Tolli..."

I clambered out of Tempus Aurora, and Alex followed me. We were battered and bruised from the abrupt landing, but not seriously harmed. I quickly examined the time machine; it appeared unscathed and fully functional.

I repeated to myself, "It should have worked."

But I couldn't figure out what had gone wrong.

As I ran toward the door leading to the hallway, Alex shouted, "Wren! Where are you going?"

"To find our friends," I yelled back, but I hesitated when I noticed he wasn't following me.

As my eyes focused on his face, I could see the despair clearly displayed in his blue eyes.

"There's no point."

I knew he was probably right, but I couldn't accept it. I couldn't stop fighting against the weight of pain and loss threatening to crash down on me. It wasn't right. This wasn't how it was supposed to end.

I argued, "Maybe it is hopeless, but there's no point in staying here, Alex. I know our plan failed. But, I'm not waiting around to fade away into nothingness, even if we can't do anything to stop it. You can stay here if you want, or you can come with me to find Cass and Tolli to see if they're okay...I know Rob wouldn't want us to just sit here."

Alex sighed, glanced back at the time machine, then nodded at me. The two of us hurried out the door and raced down the shadowy hallways that led to the infirmary wing. As we ran, the roar of a fierce wind, like a massive tornado, began to form. It slammed against the building's walls, causing the solid concrete to crack and warp perilously.

"Wren, this place is coming down!" Alex yelled as a light fixture fell near him, and the fluorescent tube exploded with a loud pop.

It sent flying shards of thin glass dangerously close to him, and he raised his arms and ducked his head instinctively.

We kept sprinting side by side, even though we both knew our actions were pointless. The end was inevitable, but I stubbornly refused to think of what would come next. My will to survive overpowered reason and doubt. Rob's final words rang in my ears, and I wouldn't let go of them. They were all I had left of the man who had been like a father to me. I winced, remembering his blank, lifeless eyes and tried to push the image out of the forefront of my mind.

I just needed to find Cass and Tolli.

I focused on the rhythm of my heartbeat and regulating my breathing. I concentrated on every step I took as we turned each corner. We sped by frightened people, and my heart ached at the thought of the fear growing in everyone awakened by the storm. They had no idea of the magnitude of the coming devastation.

Angry, dark clouds suddenly rolled across the sky, smothering any rays of moonlight coming in through the windows. The fluorescent lights above us that had already gone out sparked and crackled.

Outside, bolts of purple and indigo lightning leapt between the clouds ominously, bathing the dark halls in an eerie violet glow. A flash of lightning exploded close to us, and thunder crashed menacingly overhead, sending reverberations through the walls, floor, and ceiling. I put up my arms to cover my head.

Around us, panicked people shouted in pure terror and huddled together. Another group ran by, disoriented and confused. Alex and I held onto each other to steady ourselves.

"Alex?"

His shoulders slouched. "I think it's over, Wren."

We stumbled into a large space. I squinted and pointed at two familiar figures at the other end. "There! Cass, Tolli—I see them!"

Cass and Tolli had their backs to us and didn't hear me yelling. I assumed they hadn't been able to find a doctor, but then I saw that the hallway they needed to go through was blocked. The ceiling had collapsed, and splintered wooden beams stuck out of the rubble. The few people left cleared out of the area, but it looked like Cass and Tolli were still surveying the wreckage to see if they could find a way through.

My gaze was wrenched away from Cass and Tolli, and drawn to the scene that played out behind them through the large shattered window. A sudden flash in the thick, swirling clouds blinded me, and I tried to blink away the glowing spots that danced across my vision.

When my eyesight cleared a few seconds later, I saw bolts of electricity striking horizontally into the middle of the clouds, forming a growing violet spiral in the heart of the storm. It reminded me of the unnatural blue lightning that haunted my dreams, but this was different. The lightning wasn't striking down toward land; it collected and swirled in a funnel. This was like nothing I had ever seen before.

My eyes widened as a black hole opened in the centre of the shifting clouds, and flashes of lightning dispersed at the edges. Out of the darkness, a shining beam of light broke through. It began to grow, swerving toward us as if some unseen force was drawing it in. My attention turned to Cass and Tolli, who finally noticed us and waved, unaware of what was happening behind them.

The violet light rapidly grew larger and brighter, and I jumped into Alex, knocking us both to the ground. I had a split second to look up before the streak of light collided with the side of the building. I shielded my face with my arms as Alex and I were propelled backward against the wall. I slammed into the concrete as a part of the ceiling gave out, exploding in a cloud of dust. I crashed to the floor, and everything went dark.

In a daze, I rolled onto my side and felt the stinging of bits of glass and debris embedded into my exposed skin. I clutched my ribs as a sharp pain stabbed my chest. When I closed my eyes, I saw the explosion and the mysterious purple light as vividly as when it had happened. My heart pounded in my ears, and I became aware of the strong taste of iron in my mouth. I brought my hand to my lips and wiped away the blood before pushing my tangled hair out of my face.

I forced myself to my feet and looked over at Alex, who lay on his back next to me. His hair and face were covered in fine white dust, and cuts were scattered across his caramel-brown forearms. Scarlet streaks smeared the side of his face and seeped from a small, jagged wound near his hairline.

"Alex! Alex, are you hurt?"

His eyes remained closed, and he didn't move. Icy fear pierced my heart, and a faded glimpse of Alex bleeding out on the floor of Cyril's fortress replayed in my mind, taunting me and reminding me that I couldn't save my friends.

No matter what I did, the people I loved suffered.

I struggled to breathe as the painful memories continued to gnaw away at me, triggering the growing desire to give up and accept my fate. I heard Xavi's gun go off over and over in my head. I saw Alex's body crumpling to the floor, and I clamped my hands over my ears and squeezed my eyes shut.

"Please stop," I whimpered.

A voice answered hoarsely, "What?"

My head snapped up. I lowered my arms and scrambled closer to Alex. I noticed the subtle rising and falling of his chest.

"Alex? Please answer me. Are you okay? Are you hurt?"

"Yes," he groaned, "no...I don't know." He eased himself onto his elbows, inhaling sharply, and he raised a hand to his temple. "Ouch. Maybe a little bit."

As the dust cloud enveloping us dissipated, I helped Alex up and stared at the huge hole in the roof showing the starry sky. The storm clouds had dispersed. The moonlight illuminated the charred and smoking edges, and the jagged remains of metal pipes and wooden beams stuck out at odd angles, like sharp teeth.

As I scanned the dark room, I cupped my hands around my mouth and shouted, "Cass! Tolli!"

Alex and I staggered forward and carefully navigated through the hazardous wreckage to avoid further injury. Chunks of bricks and mortar littered the floor, only visible due to the bright moon. I followed Alex up a large pile of rubble that overlooked the remains of the room we had been in a short time ago. Everything was coated with a layer of dust, including me, and I held my side as each cough caused pain to ripple through my body.

Alex suddenly pointed to our left. "Wren, over there!"

We cautiously jumped down. But, there was nowhere we could go. The world was deteriorating all around us along with our broken timeline.

"I'll help Tolli. You find Vee," Alex ordered as he rushed over to Tolli's side.

Tolli was mostly buried by debris. Only his head and one arm were visible as he struggled to try to free himself. As Alex began pushing away the lumber and concrete that threatened to crush Tolli, I continued to look for Cass.

It seemed hopeless as I surveyed what I could make out in the dim light. The extent of the destruction spread in every direction, but I pressed on until I heard a familiar voice yelling from the other side of the windowsill. I hurried over and found her clinging to the frame, dangling by her fingertips. The wave of energy must have flung her through the window.

I quickly grabbed Cass's arm, aware that we were many stories up, and a fall would be fatal. Terror flashed in her gray eyes, and I held onto her firmly with all the strength left in my body.

I tightened my grip on both of her arms as she pushed against the window ledge with her legs. Through clenched jaws, I told her, "I'm not going to let you die."

As soon as I pulled her onto solid ground, she rolled over onto her back and gulped down a few deep breaths. "Thanks, Wren. Could this day get any crazier?"

Cass slowly stood up and dusted off her sleeves and pants as Alex and Tolli walked over.

Tolli bent forward and rubbed his chest. "Man, I thought my ribs were going to stab my lungs. It felt like an elephant was sitting on me."

He winced and put his other hand on his head. "Oh, my head…everything is spinning," he moaned before turning around and vomiting on the ground.

A small gasp escaped my lips, and Alex put a hand on his friend's back. "Hey, buddy, you okay? I think you hit your head really hard."

Tolli wiped his mouth on his ripped sleeve, and I noticed the goose egg on his forehead and a deep cut across his arm. His pants were torn, showing scrapes from where he had been pinned under fallen debris. His ratty hair, like Alex's, was covered in white dust.

"Uh…I'm not sure. I think I hit my whole body, but I think I'm okay. Good thing my head cushioned the blow."

Even at a time like this, Tolli attempted to lighten the mood.

"Wait, why are you guys here?" Cass questioned, keeping an eye on Tolli. "Where's Mallick? Are we out of the time loop?"

The foundations of the facility shifted violently, and we all wobbled and fell as we tried to keep our balance. Staying seated, Alex started to explain things to Cass and Tolli.

I barely heard him as my mind spun. In a daze, I watched as Cass started crying, and Tolli's expression hardened when Alex filled them in on Rob's death. I couldn't deal with the grief, so I rose to my feet and walked away. There would be another time to mourn for Rob.

Why had the timeline not reset? Why were we still fighting it?
And what was that streak of light?

⇛ TERMINUS TERRA COMPLETE

October 2, 2059, ?...

My gaze wandered to the crater directly below the hole in the roof. It had made an enormous cavern down to the first floor. I felt an irresistible pull toward it and cautiously shuffled closer to the edge. When I saw the violet glow coming from the centre, my heart skipped a few beats.

It suddenly felt like I had been removed from my body, and I was watching myself do something I knew was dangerous, but had no ability to stop.

I lowered myself over the edge of the crater. I descended deeper, using sturdy chunks of concrete and metal pipes as handholds and footholds. Down, down, down. I was mesmerized by the light at the bottom. As I dropped down, glass, drywall, mortar, and concrete crunched under my weight.

It felt surreal as I walked closer to the centre of the wreckage, focused on finding the source. Everyone and everything else melted away. I found myself bending down and letting my hand hover over what appeared to be another orb.

Except this one wasn't blue. It was a deep, beautiful violet.

There was a familiar aura surrounding the mysterious object. The soft glow of the orb captivated my entire being and made it impossible for me to tear my eyes away. It was as if I could see beyond the surface of the orb, into a vast expanse that could only be described as the deep purple of space. I hesitated to touch the dark twin of the blue orb, and I drew my hand back quickly as haunting images of my past flashed in my mind. For a moment, I doubted every decision I made after the accident that changed my life.

But, something felt different about this orb, and I couldn't resist it. Impulsively, I picked it up. It was cool to the touch, and the weight of it surprised me.

Without warning, a long-forgotten but familiar voice rang out, "Wren, are you there?"

The voice startled me, causing me to inadvertently drop the orb. To my surprise, on impact with the ground, it began broadcasting a hologram of a man. He had shaggy, white-blonde hair and a friendly, wide grin on his lips. Dark bags sagged under his unmistakably blue eyes.

He looked the same as the day he died.

My throat constricted as my jaw hung open, and I gasped for air. I had to pinch myself hard to make sure I wasn't dreaming.

My dead uncle's image, tinted by a soft violet hue, shone brightly in front of me. His eyes sparkled with excitement as he spoke loudly, "Wren, is that you? Can you hear me?"

I squeezed my eyes shut, wondering if I was hallucinating, but also hoping against all odds that my uncle had survived all those years ago.

But that was impossible. Impossible! Had I finally gone over the edge?

I clenched my fists and hesitantly opened my eyes, but the life-sized image of William Derecho remained, projecting directly out of the dark purple orb. By this time, Alex, Tolli, and Cass had slid down into the crater and stood next to me.

"Wren! Alex! It's me, William. Please answer if you can hear me. Time is of the essence!"

The four of us stood in stunned silence with matching bewildered expressions at the unbelievable scene set out before us. I was jolted out of my trance as the foundations threateningly creaked underfoot, serving as a reminder that time was truly running out.

"And is that Trevor and Cassandra?" My uncle's hologram squinted. "The image isn't clear on this end. I've been looking for the four of you!"

"William Derecho," Alex whispered, his face filled with shock. "How is this possible? You died two years ago. There's no way…"

His voice faltered at the end as he tried to choke back his emotions. I knew by the look on his face we were both thinking about the day Uncle William died. Alex hadn't witnessed his death, but I had watched every horrifying moment.

I caught a glimpse of his face through the small window.

Fear and pain filled Uncle William's pale-blue eyes as flames consumed the time machine. He desperately banged on the doors, and I stood, paralyzed. It was not supposed to be this way. Tempus wasn't ready to be tested yet.

The smoke from the charred hole in my jean pocket overwhelmed my senses. The orb had burned right through the fabric, and I looked down to see it slowly rolling toward the machine. I didn't have time to react when the blue, otherworldly lightning entered through the hole in the roof, weaving its way down to the orb.

The orb: the root of so much pain in my life.

The split second seemed to stretch out as the lightning extended its thin fingers to touch the smooth, alluring sphere. The blast threw me backward, causing my head to snap back, but as I flew through the air, I caught one last glimpse of my uncle.

He would die if no one helped him. He would die if *I* didn't help him.

My body slammed into the wall, and I fell to the ground. I tasted blood and groaned as I lay there on the floor, trying to process what had just happened. My whole body throbbed with a dull pain, but, surprisingly, as I rolled onto my side, nothing felt broken.

So strange.

Floating in and out of consciousness, I struggled to block out the lingering image of Tempus engulfed in flames. I kept seeing Uncle William's face. Blood-curdling screams deafened me, and I was aware that I couldn't move my hands to cover my ears.

Eventually, my eyelids fluttered open as I fought to fully regain my senses. There was nothing where Tempus once stood. All that remained were broken, blackened pieces of the time machine scattered around me. That was it: only twisted metal scraps.

But, I had seen his face.

In Uncle William's last moment alive, I had thought I'd seen his eyes flash a brighter shade of blue. At the time, though, I thought nothing of it. I only felt the consuming agony that threatened to tear my heart in two.

My uncle was dead. I would never be the same.

"Maybe it's a pre-recorded message?" Alex mumbled, puzzled.

"No, Alex. I'm very much alive," Uncle William said firmly and glanced over his shoulder at something we couldn't see. "We have a lot of catching up to do, but listen to me when I say that we don't have much time."

As if to prove his point, the holographic image flickered threateningly in and out.

"I don't understand. He's supposed to be dead," Tolli insisted roughly, stepping closer. His body swayed, and Cass reached out to help him. He leaned on her shoulder, gasping in pain. "How in the world can he be here as a ghost projecting out of that weird purple…light thing? Can someone please tell me what is going on?"

Cass chimed in. "Yeah, what Tolli said."

"I think we all need an explanation," Alex suggested.

"The Keeper can only transmit interdimensionally for so long. Listen, Wren, use the violet orb to power the time machine," Uncle William commanded. "I'll have time to explain everything after, but, for now, you need to focus on this one thing." His gaze flicked to Alex, then Cass, and finally to Tolli. "All four of you have to stay together. Find Rob Mallick. You need to convince him to come with you. He can explain more later. Get everyone inside Tempus, and I'll take care of the rest."

I hesitantly turned to look at each of my friends. Cass had a blank look in her gray eyes, and Tolli's brow was furrowed. Alex subconsciously swept away the hair poking his eyes as his focus bounced between the image of Uncle William and the violet orb in the middle of the crater. None of us said anything about Rob.

I took a deep breath. "We have to do what he says. We have to go."

"Wren, are you sure about this?" Alex bit his lip.

I shook my head. "No, but what other choice do we have?"

"This seems highly suspicious, if you ask me." Tolli narrowed his eyes at the hologram.

"Yeah, how does he even know me? And what about everyone else?" Cass asked, and her eyes widened as she struggled to face the moral consequences of abandoning the people she cared about. "Addy? Irving? Silvia Mercier? Director Li? They'll all die if we leave them."

Alex met her worried gaze with empathy. He reasoned, "I know we would never choose to leave them unless we had to. But, maybe if we can find a way to get out of all this safely, we can find a way to save them."

"This isn't right," she sighed, looking around helplessly before staring down at her feet.

"The alternative is doing nothing as the building collapses on top of us," I said, grabbing the violet orb and hurrying to climb out of the crater. "Then we definitely can't help anyone. Let's go!"

"All of you need to get in the time machine right now," Uncle William said, waving his arms animatedly as his image projected next to me. "You can't stay in that reality any longer. You'll all fade from existence!"

Tolli yelled out as he followed me. "Well, when you put it like that..."

The conversation was over; the decision was made. The four of us raced back to my room, dodging falling debris and leaping over cracked, crumbling concrete. Uncle William's image began to glitch, and now only crackling fragments of sentences were being transmitted through the violet orb.

"...Protectors...stay together...Mallick..."

I had so many questions, but I knew I needed to get to my uncle first before I would get answers.

As we entered my room, I slid to my knees and reached into the heart of Amelia's disc to wrench out the blue orb and toss it aside. It rolled toward Alex's feet and stopped right in front of him as he stared down at it.

"Leave it! We don't need that cursed thing anymore!"

"Wren, are you sure?" There was an uncertainty in his voice. "You told me about everything your future self could do with...Don't you think we might find a use for it? Or at least keep it from people who would misuse it?"

"If it's the cause of all this, it has to stay here and be erased from existence with everything else. There's something evil about it...I don't even know what to believe right now, but I don't want anything to do with that orb ever again."

I rose to my feet, but Alex didn't budge. He stared down at the orb resting by his boot. It seemed to pulse and radiate heat.

I persisted, "It has no control over me—over anyone anymore."

"Then, you know you can resist it. You're the only one who can handle it."

"Alex, I tried to destroy it once, and it didn't work. I don't want to be tied to it anymore." I stepped up to him and squeezed his hand. "Trust me. As for us, we need to leave."

Alex smiled softly at me and nodded. His blue eyes didn't seem to bother me as much as they first did. I turned away from him to attach the dark orb in its place, and Uncle William's glitching hologram vanished. I climbed into the time machine.

"That's not going to fit us all," Tolli pointed out as Cass slipped inside Tempus Aurora after me. "I think it's only meant for one person."

"Just squish in," I ordered him. "Unless you want to see what a collapsed reality looks like."

Tolli shrugged. "Yessir."

He awkwardly pushed himself in on the other side of me, and I glanced over my shoulder. "Alex?"

Alex slammed Tempus Aurora's door shut behind him, sealing the four of us in. "I'm here. Let's go."

He leaned on the back of my seat, his shoulders bumping both Cass and Tolli. Cass flattened against the control desk as Tolli tried to squeeze farther into the corner.

Without any of us touching anything, Tempus Aurora started up by itself. The control console began to glow the same dark purple as the orb that powered it. Uncle William's voice crackled through the speaker, "…Keepers…needs help…be here soon."

Before we could take off, violent tremors shook the building, and Cass crashed into me. Tolli yelped as his head banged against metal behind me while Alex gripped the back of my seat, trying to brace himself.

It felt like we were being shaken in a bottle. To make matters worse, the ceiling of my room began to give way. Large chunks of white drywall rained down on us, covering the round windows with dust and obscuring our ability to see what was happening outside.

"Hey, Mr. William's ghost, sir, now's a great time to get us outta here," Tolli shouted as he tried his best to hold onto the machine's smooth walls.

A burst of static overwhelmed the speaker, accompanied by a few more cryptic words from Uncle William, "…put you in a time loop…not on Terra."

Now, I was more confused than ever, and my mind churned with questions.

Maybe the time loop wasn't my fault after all? But if the orb also didn't initiate it, who or what did? How could my uncle not be dead, let alone not be on the only planet in the solar system inhabited by humans? Where else could he be? Who were "The Keepers"? And what did it have to do with the dark-purple orb?

I finally asked the question we'd all been wondering, "Then where are we going?"

The foundations of the enormous complex crumbled, and the portal opened beneath us just in time. As we began to plummet down into the depths of space, Uncle William's final word echoed throughout Tempus Aurora.

"Earth."

EPILOGUE: UNKNOWN

Again, you tried to destroy me.

Again, you thought you could leave me behind.

Your mistake.

You gambled with your planet and lost.

Have you learned nothing?

Do you still believe you can defeat me and alter your fate?

I am power.

I am control.

I am The Protector.

And I will save my world.

My world, plagued with war stretching beyond time.

My plans are set.

And I am patient.

I am in the shadows.

And I will always prevail.

"Phase Two: assets identified and extracted. Time loop broken. Mission complete."

Welcome to Earth.

ACKNOWLEDGEMENTS

THANK YOU to everyone who made a huge deal over my first book! I was blown away by all the support.

Extra special thanks to my mom and dad, Jeamie and Chris Nichol. You guys are the best, and this book wouldn't have been possible without you. Thank you for all the hours you put into brainstorming and editing with me.

Thank you to Common Deer Press, especially Kirsten Marion, who did an amazing job with the editing. I'm so glad I had the opportunity to publish my second book with you. Thanks to Jennifer Foster, who did the copy edits. Also, thanks to David Moratto for another beautiful cover.

One of the coolest things about living in Cold Lake is getting to know all the fighter pilots. Thank you to Capt Stephen "Krako" Kane, for helping me make the air battle scene more realistic and accurate. I loved how it turned out! Thanks for taking the time to answer all my questions.

Thanks to my extended family for their love and support. Thanks to my grandparents, Kai and Eliza Kwan, and Cecil and Normie Nichol. Thank you, Uncle Jamie and Auntie Renee, Uncle Kevin and Auntie Cheryl, Uncle Cam and Auntie Janelle, Auntie Shauna, and all my amazing cousins.

Thanks Mr. Yoshida and all the kids in my Social 20-1 class ("academic elite"). I looked forward to coming to class every day as you blared music from your room. I hope your cheese bagels don't catch on fire... again.

Thanks Mrs. Cherniwchan and all the kids in my PE 20 class. We had a lot of fun playing basketball! Contrary to popular belief, we were not cursed...

Thanks to my brothers, Silas and Titus, and my sister, Everett, who make me laugh so hard all the time. Especially Titus, who sometimes wears his underwear backwards...and inside out. You guys are awesome, and I couldn't ask for better siblings.

ABOUT THE AUTHOR

Nyah Nichol was born and raised in Cold Lake, Alberta, where she currently attends Cold Lake High School. A few of her many hobbies are reading, playing her ukulele, crocheting, climbing, and doing anything artsy. She has three younger siblings who can be annoying at times, but sweet, awesome, and very entertaining the rest of the time. She has an amazing mom and dad who love her very much and support her in everything she does.